FANCY

When I despair, I remember that all through history the way of truth and love have always won. There have been tyrants and murderers, and for a time, they can seem invincible, but in the end, they always fall. Think of it…always.

Gandhi

FANCY

Advantage
BOOKS

MICHAEL EDWIN Q.

Fancy by Michael Edwin Q.
Copyright © 2019 by Michael Edwin Q.
All Rights Reserved.
ISBN: 978-1-59755-540-1

Published by: ADVANTAGE BOOKS™
                  Longwood, Florida, USA
                  www.advbookstore.com

Library of Congress Catalog Number: 2019948057
1.   Fiction:: African American - Woman
2.   Fiction: African American – Historical
3.   Social Science - Slavery

Cover Design: Alexander von Ness
Edited by: Nancy E. Sabitini

First Printing: September 2019
19 20 21 22 23 24   10 9 8 7 6 5 4 3 2 1
Printed in the United States of America

One

Nearly a Fancy

"Jolene…Jolene…prettiest gal I ever seen."

It had been sung to her every day of her life by her parents, from the cradle to petticoats, with good cause, too. At the age of thirteen, she was the most beautiful young woman in Lexington, Kentucky, black or white. She could turn the head of any man, young or old, no matter what his race. Even her slavery sat upon her like a crown.

She was petite in stature, delicate in nature. There was a womanly shapeliness, most girls of her age would not know for many more years. Doe eyes seemingly resting upon her high cheekbones, lips like two rose petals. Her tiny hands remained soft, unblemished, despite whatever slave labor needed to be preformed, rebelling against natural law. Always their first comment, what most folks noticed was the lightness of her skin, which was immaculately even and smooth.

However, there was one other of Jolene's features most folks would not notice at a glance. You would have to get to know her to be aware of it. Folks talk about beauty being only skin-deep. As it was with Jolene, she was even more beautiful within, shining like a flame bringing light to her outer beauty. She was a warm, sweet young woman. Her kindness poured out to everyone she came in contact with, be it family, friend, or enemy. Everyone knew her as a giving person with always a kind word, always willing to help.

As for her outer beauty, she never seemed aware of it, never flaunting it or wheeling it like a sword as most folks would do. Despite being so blessed, Jolene was more concerned with laying blessings on others.

Finally, at the center of all this was her heart. She remained as innocent as the day she was born, an innocence rarely seen in folks. Though being her crowning glory, it would be a source of much sorrow for many years. Yet, even if she knew of such things to come, she would not nor could she change her ways.

The Barnett Plantation was no better or worse than any other plantation, which is a falsehood only other plantation owners believed for any plantation with slave labor is a pit in hell.

Jolene worked in the fields alongside her father and mother, Truman and Lillian Fairchild, third generation slaves. After many years of marriage, childless, they had Jolene, a blessing to a forgotten prayer. Up in years, they knew Jolene would be their only child, they showered her with attention, love and sensible Biblical guidance, though neither one could read. Still, there is much to learn from word of mouth.

As she blossomed into a woman, many were the eyes of young men that wandered over her, coveting. This is understandable, as it always has been, as it should be. The overseers and white workers on the plantation were not immune. Their eyes roved over her like wolves eyeing a newborn lambkin. Except it was all look and no touch. Despite all appearances, a slave is property. Jolene was not their property to claim. Any man so much as touching her inappropriately would have to answer to Garland Barnett, owner of the plantation and of Jolene. Overstepping your bounds, a man could only hope for just the loss of his job, as Garland Barnett was known for his temper, dealing out his own form of justice with either fists or pistol.

As like Truman and Lillian Fairchild, Garland was third generation, except as a plantation owner. In his youth, Garland envisioned a family life with a wife and many children. This was not to be. True; he married Doreen Covington, the daughter of a wealthy tobacco baron. She was the love of his youth and of his life. Sadly, she died in childbirth. Garland never considered being with another woman, though rumor was he made monthly visits to a sporting club in town whenever the mood was upon him.

Despite the loss of his wife, Garland rejoiced in his son, Henry, in whom he placed all his concern and hope. An heir assured another generation of Barnett would rule.

Many the friend warned Garland of spoiling his son. However, he didn't see it as such. To him it was a way of preparing him to own and run the plantation. If the boy lived a life without want, believing life must always go his way; there would be no stopping him. He would be a force to be reckoned with. For all purposes of owning and running a plantation, this was true, only, at what cost? Garland had created a beast with no heart, having just enough soul to stay alive and nothing more.

At first glance, one wouldn't believe Henry to be the monster he truly was. At sixteen, he was tall, dark-haired, handsome, always well-mannered, and smart as a whip.

Although, his good looks were nothing more than a façade, his polite manners were a cover-up; his intelligence was used only for self-benefit. All those, except his father, feared the young man, having as little contact with him as possible, keeping their distance.

There was not a young miss at school or within the parish that did not fancy Henry. This meant nothing to Henry, save for the joy of leading them on, playing with their hearts.

No matter, a young man's eye seldom looks for love as much as it does lust. Henry's licentious eye fixed on Jolene; he intended to have her.

****

In Jolene's world of innocence, none of this existed. Oh, she was not oblivious to evil. She had seen its many faces in her short life. How could anyone not, as a slave on a plantation? Only, she saw this as the exception, not the norm.

Jolene went about her daily business of work and play, family life and social. She never suspected Henry hid on the sideline of her world, his passion growing like a stoked fire, till finally it was too much for him to bear. He'd wait in the shadows for the right time and then strike.

It was the end of a long hard day for the Fairchild family. Getting up in years, Jolene's parents relied on her more and more.

"Your daddy's had a rough day," her mother said, handing her an empty bucket. "Be a dear, fetch us some water?"

The slave quarters were close to the fields they worked, rows of rundown shacks, mostly one room and small. In the center of the compound was a well that everyone drew from.

There were no other people around; everyone had settled in for the night. Darkness moved over the earth, Jolene walked slowly and carefully, carrying the bucket. At the well, she attached a rope to it, letting it drop. The splash echoed through the silence. It took all her strength to bring the full bucket up. When she did, she untied the rope, taking hold of the handle.

Suddenly, two strong arms encircled her from behind. She dropped the bucket back down into the well. Just as she was about to take in a deep breath to let out a scream, a hand came up, covering her mouth.

Whoever it was, they were far stronger than she. Though she struggled, she couldn't break loose. They pulled her so quickly, she couldn't get her footing. Her heels dug furrows in the dirt.

Looking downward, Jolene caught a glimpse of the hand over her mouth. It was the hand of a white man.

He dragged her away from the slave quarters to the barn. The door was open; he shoved her inside, slamming the door behind him.

A lit hurricane lamp hung from a post. It gave off just enough light to see, the small flickering flame creating long dancing shadows.

Jolene spun around, facing her assailant.

"Master Henry!" she cried in surprise.

Before she could say another word, he gave her the back of his hand, hard across her cheek. Her knees went weak. Just as she tried to regain her balance, he pushed her down onto a pile of hay. The next instant, he fell down on top of her. He wasn't a large boy, yet his weight kept her pinned under him. Fighting back as best she could, kicking, punching him, he was too strong for her.

Henry brought his face down, sealing his lips to hers. She thrashed about under him, desperately struggling to breath. She got hold of his lower lip in her mouth, biting down. He screamed, backed away, punching her several times in the face. The world began to swim in a circle.

He brought his lips down again. She could taste his blood in her mouth. His hands were all about her, grabbing her flesh at parts of her body no one ever touched. She kicked up her feet, trying to stop him from lifting the hem of her skirt.

"No, please, don't," she pleaded to deaf ears.

Eventually, it all became too much for her, as her energy faded. She could fight no more. All she could do was sob. When he got her skirt hiked up to her waist, she felt his weight lift from her. She opened her eyes to see him floating three feet above her. Was it a miracle?

Then she saw him, Garland Barnett, Henry's father. He was holding the boy by the seat of his pants and the nape of his neck. He tossed him off to the next pile of hay.

"Get in the house," Garland ordered his son.

"But, Daddy…" Henry griped

"Get in the house," Garland repeated with more force.

The boy tucked his tail between his legs, leaving the barn.

"Get up," Garland ordered Jolene. "Go home, and don't you dare tell anyone what happened. If you do, I'll kill you and your whole family. You understand?"

"Yes, sir," Jolene wept, lowering the hem of her skirt. Somehow she made it to her feet. She was shaking with fear. She left the barn.

When she entered her home, she was still flustered.

"Where ya been, girl? Ya had us worried," her mother said. Then both her parents got a better look at her when she stepped into the light.

"Good Lord, what happened to ya face?" her father asked, reaching out to her.

Jolene quickly turned her face away. "It's nothing," she said. "It was just so dark outside; I tripped and hit my head on the side of the well. I'm sorry, but I accidentally lost the bucket down the well."

"That ain't no never-mind," her mother said. "Sit down, let me clean those cuts."

****

Back at the house, Garland sat his son down. He poured them both a brandy. Taking the glass, Henry shot a confusing look at his father. This was a mixed signal. For one thing, his father never allowed him hard drink, saying he was still too young. As well, he figured his father was angry with him for what he did, or tried to do, in the barn.

Garland reached across the table, clinking glasses. Once they both took a sip, Garland smiled. "I'm not angry with you, Henry."

This confused the boy even more.

"Daddy, I don't understand. This is our plantation. These are our slaves, our property. We should be able to do with our property whatever we want to."

"You're right, son," Garland replied. "I told you I'm not angry. I saw you push that girl into the barn. I knew what you were up to, and I believe it is your right to do so. Except, when I thought about it, it gave me an idea. You...who could have any of the slave girls on this plantation...picked Jolene. Why...I asked myself. 'Cause she's one of the most desirable women around, black or white.

"I didn't stop you because I was angry. I just can't see us throwing good money away."

"Money, what money...?" Henry asked.

"There are plenty of wealthy gentlemen who'd pay good money for a virgin like her. If I let you deflower her, she'd be useless to us. As well, if I let her go marry one of the other slaves, all we'd have is a bunch of pretty babies, and that ain't any good, either. Now, I know a man who'd buy a *Nearly a Fancy*."

"Nearly a Fancy…?" Henry questioned.

"They're called *Fancy Girls*. Women who are trained to make a man happy, but it don't come natural, they must be taught. Before they become a *Fancy Lady* they are called *Nearly a Fancy*."

Garland could tell his son wasn't getting the full gist.

"You see, son, a man is like a bee. He needs to go from blossom to blossom. The bee don't care what color the flower is, neither does a man care about the color of the women he's with. Of course, you don't get serious with the dark ones. It's not a question of love, and especially not marriage. That's for women of your own kind. Someday you'll find a good woman and have a family of your own. Till then, like the bee, gather as many flowers as you can, whatever the color."

Garland poured them both another drink.

"Now, as for Jolene, she is a rare flower. A flower some bee would gladly pay a high price to own. So, you see, son, I wasn't upset about what you were doing. You don't want to cut off your nose to spite your face. There's money to be made."

Henry didn't want to admit it; the whiskey was getting to him. His head was swimming with his fathers words.

"I tell you what," Garland continued. "Is there any other slave girl you fancy?"

Henry thought for a minute, only he didn't have to think hard.

"The one called Katherine. She's not as good looking as Jolene, but she'll do."

Garland laughed, again, he clinked his glass to his son's.

"Well then, Henry, let us go down to the compound, and bring the girl here to spend the night with you. Maybe, while we're at it, I'll grab me one, too."

They downed their drinks in one gulp. They rose from their chairs, leaving the main house for the slave quarters.

Two

Diamond in the Rough

Samuel Runt dealt in slave trade. Not the normal exchange, mind you. He didn't run or own an auction house. His was a specialty service, selling the highest quality slaves to the wealthiest of slaveowners, people who wanted and could afford the very best.

His stock and trade were large male slaves who could do the work of three men. They were also good as breeders. Female slaves that were good with children were always in demand. His most popular offering was the female slave who could cook, doing domestic work, as well. Butlers and maids were needed by every home of the wealthy. Lastly, was the need for Fancy Girls. These were beautiful slave women used to entertain gentlemen of quality. These, always the highest priced, brought in the highest profit.

Runt was a tall man, slender, boney like a skeleton covered with a thin layer of skin. His profile came to a sharp hatchet-like point at the end was his long protruding nose. Always dressed in a black suit, at first glance one might think him an undertaker.

"Cigar…?" Garland asked, holding a small open cedar box across his desk to Runt.

"Don't mind if I do," Runt said, taking two cigars, placing them in his coat pocket. "I'll just save them for later," Runt remarked. This was a lie. Runt didn't smoke. He would sell them to someone who did. This was not unusual for Runt who could pinch a penny till Lady Liberty hollered for mercy.

"Brandy…?" Garland asked, holding up a bottle.

"Yes, thank you," Runt replied. His eyes went wide. He liked drinking, except whiskey cost money, so he seldom drank. Still, when offered or when someone else was buying, Runt was drinking.

"So, Mr. Barnett, tell me about this girl you want to sell?"

"Mr. Runt, what can I say? You have to see her to understand what I'm talking about."

"I'd like that," Runt said, sipping his brandy. "What makes you think she'd be a good Fancy Girl?"

"Again, seeing is believing, Mr. Runt. She's just turned thirteen, fresh as a flower." Of course, Garland had no idea what Jolene's age was, however the number thirteen sounded young enough to be alluring and old enough to not sound like you were robbing the cradle.

"Then she's a virgin?" Runt asked.

"Most definitely, as fresh as December snow, and untouched. Have another brandy, Mr. Runt?"

"Don't mind if I do," Runt said, holding his glass out to Barnett.

Just then, there was a knock at the door. It slowly opened.

"Ya wanted to see me, sir?" Jolene asked as she entered.

"This is the girl I was telling you about." Barnett told Runt.

Runt looked her up and down.

"What is your name, child?" he asked.

"Jolene, sir…"

Runt looked to Barnett, "It's a pretty name. At least we won't have to change it."

This puzzled Jolene, however, her facial expression was more of fear than confusion.

Runt rose from his seat, slowly walking around Jolene, inspecting her from head to toe, as if she were cattle.

"Open your mouth, girl," he demanded.

Jolene looked at him strangely; the request took her off guard.

"I said, 'open your mouth'; I want to see your teeth."

Jolene opened her mouth.

"Wider…wider, that's good," he said looking into her mouth, both up and down. "Her teeth are all there and they look good," Runt told Barnett, sounding impressed. "Tell me, girl, do you clean your teeth?"

"Yes, sir, everyday I use sackcloth dipped in water and salt."

"That's good," he said, returning to his seat. He pointed to her feet. "Lift up your skirt," he commanded.

"Excuse me, sir?"

"I want you to lift your skirt. I want to see your legs." Runt turned to Barnett. "Make her lift her skirt."

"You heard the man," Barnett growled.

Jolene took hold of her skirt, lifting the hem.

"Higher…higher…above the knees," Runt insisted.

Jolene did as she was told. Her body shaking, head bowed down with shame.

"That's enough," Runt said.

Jolene lowered her skirt, letting out a sigh of relief.

"Well, Mr. Runt, isn't she everything I told you she was?" Barnett inquired as he poured them both another brandy.

"She is a lovely child," Runt agreed. "But…"

"But what…?

"Well, to be honest, she's a diamond in the rough. She needs polishing. Much work needs to be done. Wealthy gentlemen want to spend time with women of quality, who are well-groomed; can hold a conversation, which can read and write. This girl is as uncouth as a jackass. It will take months and much money to get her up to snuff. With that in mind, I can only offer you five-hundred dollars."

"I can get three-hundred for an old hag," Barnett argued. "I'll take no less than one-thousand dollars."

Runt had set a trap; Barnett blindly fell into it. He knew Jolene was worth far more than five-hundred. In fact, he would have been willing to go as high as two thousand. But he knew five-hundred would be an insult. He wanted to rile Barnett, get his blood hot. An angry man doesn't think straight. To save face, Barnett spurted out the first number to come into his head, half of what Runt was willing to pay.

Runt took his time, making grueling faces, as if he were muddling over the offer. Of course, he knew he would go for it, however, he wanted to give the appearance Barnett outsmarted him.

"Very well, one-thousand it is. I won't make any money, still, I'll make one of my customers happy, which will pay off in the long run." This too was a lie. Runt would make a small fortune on Jolene.

After money exchanged, papers signed, the two men shook hands.

"Jolene, Mr. Runt is now your new Massa. Do as you're told, make me proud, girl."

"Come, my dear, my carriage is outside and ready. We leave immediately," Runt announced.

It was then the full weight of what happened crashed down upon Jolene.

"But…?"

"No buts, girl, come along."

Jolene fell to her knees at Runt's feet, her hands clasped together, praying for mercy.

"Please, sir, don't do this! I'm just a child!"

"I know," Runt laughed. "Isn't it wonderful?"

"But my parents, please, sir, let me at least say good-bye to my parents."

"No time for that. We need to catch a train."

Jolene burst out crying, tears streaming down her cheeks.

"Please, sir, I'm a good girl, please don't do this!"

Poor girl didn't understand how some people can be. She shot her pleas at Runt's heart, only to miss it by a mile, for it was such a small target, indeed. Instead, he found it amusing, and dare I say it, aroused his passions. He smiled, realizing he had made a very good buy. There would be much money to make on this diamond in the rough.

****

Jolene looked blankly out the window of the train, miles of mountains, trees, lakes, and fields rushed past. Little of it registered in her mind, her thoughts were far away. Each rattle of the steel wheels along the tracks and planks took her farther from her family, friends, from the only life she knew. A pain rose in her heart she never knew to be possible. Can a person really die of heartbreak?

Runt's traveling companions were two large bodyguards who never spoke, laughed, or smiled. They sat across from her with vacant stares, watching her every moment. Any thoughts of escape were futile. Runt always sat alone.

After days of travel, they arrived at Atlanta, Georgia. Jolene never new a town could be so large, buildings to the sky, people elbow to elbow, and the clatter was frightening.

They got three rooms at the *Continental Hotel*, one room for the bodyguards, a suite for Runt, and a small room for Jolene, which they locked from the outside.

In the evening, the guards collected her, taking her upstairs. Jolene looked about in amazement. Even a palace could not be as grand.

They opened the door to one of the rooms at the end of the hall. They pushed her inside, slamming the door behind her.

"Come in, my dear," Runt said, cheerfully. "Come in."

Entering the room, Jolene was taken by the volume of it, three times the size of their entire home back on the plantation. Everything was either gold or white marble. A small table covered with plates of food stood in the center of the room.

"Sit," Runt said, still sounding friendly. "Have something to eat. You haven't eaten a thing since we left. You must be starved."

It was true. In her delirium and sorrow, she hadn't eaten in days. The aroma made it too difficult to bear. She took a seat at the table and began to eat.

Runt laughed at her. "You eat like a barbarian. But, don't worry, we'll set you straight. You're going to be a lady, once this is all over."

Jolene didn't say a word, continuing to eat.

"Would you like to know where we're going?" he asked. He didn't bother to wait for a reply. "We're going to New Orleans. Marvelous city, New Orleans, you will love it. There I will hand you over to Madam Charbonneau. She runs a school, a school for little girls just like you. She takes diamonds in the rough and makes them ladies of quality – Fancy Ladies, that is."

When Jolene finished eating, Runt took her by the arm, lifting her to her feet. They stood at the foot of his bed, both his hands holding her arms. He looked deep into her eyes.

"My God, it's a good thing I love money more than women or I'd throw you down on this bed and take you myself."

He pulled her to the door, opening it. He pushed her out into the hall, into the hands of the guards.

"Lock her in her room," Runt ordered, slamming the door.

Three

A Trace of Africa

New Orleans was as large as Atlanta, only different. If a city could be male or female, Atlanta was male, a titan. New Orleans would be feminine, a goddess. Everything was ornate, flamboyant. As the carriage drove up the hills north of the center of town, Jolene looked back, seeing the harbor full of ships. Their masts like hundreds of crucifixes bobbing up and down in the water.

It was a large property on the edge of town, surrounded by high stonewalls. There were guards at the gate. Encircled with elaborate gardens on all sides, the house was a two-story mansion with dozens of rooms. Again, there were guards at the front door.

Jolene followed Runt down the hallway to a door. He knocked. "It's Samuel," he called out.

"Come in," a woman's voice called out through the door.

Inside was part library, with book shelves on three walls, and an office with a desk in front of a large window. Behind the desk sat a woman of great beauty and grace. Her hair was dark, tight to her head, as dark as her eyes. Her skin was pearl white. She dressed like a princess. It was difficult to estimate her age, there was youthfulness in her eyes and movements, yet there was womanhood about her that only years could give.

"So, nice to see you, again," Runt said, with a slight bow.

"And you, Runt," her voice was like bells ringing, with a slight French accent. "So, this is the girl you told me about," she said, stepping around her desk toward them. Her movements were fluid and refined.

"Yes, what do you think?" Runt asked, pointing to Jolene, his hand moving from her head to toe.

"She has promise," the woman replied.

"Then I leave her in your capable hands," Runt said moving toward the door. "How long do you think it will take?" he asked.

"It's hard to say. It depends on how bad off she is and how fast she learns. We'll see. I'll write you when she's ready. However, don't expect to hear from me sooner than six months."

"Oh," Runt said, sounding disappointed. "Madam Charbonneau..." Runt declared, again, bowing slightly.

"Mr. Runt..." Madam Charbonneau responded.

Runt left the room. As soon as his footsteps faded and the front door slammed, Madam Charbonneau approached Jolene.

"What is your name, girl?"

"Jolene, ma'am..."

"You will always address me as Madam, do you understand? Here you will do everything I tell you to. In a few month's time, you will be worthy of a fine sum from a wealthy gentlemen. You should be grateful; your life has taken a turn for the better."

Madam moved closer to Jolene, reaching out to her. She caressed Jolene's cheek and then along her neck. It was a strange feeling. It made Jolene uncomfortable, it made her shiver.

"Jolene, aye...? Est-ce que tu parles François?"

"I'm sorry, Madam, I don't speak anything but what I speak."

"What a shame," Madam sighed. "You have a French name, you know? One can only hope. Oh, well. Follow me, girl."

Stepping out of the room, they stood before a wide staircase. There was a bell hanging from the wall. Madam rang it, shaking a cord tied to the clapper. Then she guided Jolene into the parlor.

Two minutes later, in walked six women. They were all well-dressed and groomed, like Madam. The first woman was older than the others who were young like Jolene. She was a large black woman, wide in the hips and shoulders. The other five were young, petite, black girls. Four of them were fair skinned, like Jolene or lighter, save for one girl who was a deep black, darker than anyone Jolene ever knew.

"This is our new student. Her name is Jolene," Madam announced.

Two of the girls smiled at Jolene, the fairest and the darkest. Another seemingly stared through her, unconcerned. The last two giggled at Jolene's backwoods look.

"Don't laugh!" Madam reprimanded. "None of you were any better than she when you first came here." Madam pointed to the older woman, as she addressed Jolene. "This is Cora, the housemother. When I'm not around, her word is law. You will obey her as you would me." She turned to Cora. "There you have it, Cora. I leave you to it."

Madam left the parlor. A moment later they heard her office door close.

"All right, girls. I want everyone to help...what was your name, again?"

"Jolene..."

"I want all of you to help Jolene these next few days." She looked to one of the girls. "Winnie, since Lucinda is no longer with us, Jolene will be your new roommate."

"Yes'um."

"All right, ladies, everyone to your rooms, I'll see you at dinner."

They all headed for the stairs.

"Come with me," Winnie said to Jolene.

They followed the others up the stairs.

The room was large, bright and clean.

"This will be your bed; these are your dresses," Winnie said, pointing to the bed farthest from the windows, and a freestanding wardrobe a few feet from the bed.

Jolene looked inside the wardrobe. "Are these all mine?" she asked, amazed at the fabrics and colors.

"Yes, they are," Winnie replied. "Only, I think it best you clean up first." She pulled a cord dangling along the far wall.

"What is this place?" Jolene asked.

Winnie laughed, "It's a finishing school for mistresses. When they feel you're ready, they'll sell you to some wealthy man, a white man, you understand?"

"But that's so wrong," Jolene argued. "That's not Christian."

"Maybe not, but it's a far better life than living and working in the fields."

Just then, the door opened, a maid stood ready.

"Run a bath," Winnie ordered. "This young lady needs one."

"Yes, miss," the maid replied, running off to make it so.

Jolene held her arm next to Winnie's.

"I thought I was light skinned. Ya could probably pass."

"Don't think I haven't tried," Winnie laughed. "Only that's why we're here. Wealthy gentlemen love that *Trace of Africa*, in a woman. They can't resist it, it drives them crazy."

"It all sounds so wrong," Jolene groaned.

Winnie laughed, again. "You'll learn. Come on; let's get you washed up, so we can both dress for dinner."

****

The dining room was long with an equally long dining table. Madam sat at the head of the table, Cora at the other end; the girls sat three on each side.

"Just follow my lead. Do whatever I do," Winnie whispered to Jolene.

In spite of all her best efforts, Jolene couldn't help doing it all wrong. The other girls smirked at her. Madam hit the side of her water glass with her butter knife, to get everyone's attention.

"That's enough of that, girls."

They muffled their laughter into their napkins.

"It would seem we have our job cut out for us," Madam said, looking across the table to Cora.

"Yes, Madam," Cora agreed.

"All right, ladies, everybody upstairs. We have a long day tomorrow," Madam announced, pushing away from the table, retiring to her bedroom, which was on the first floor.

As they all walked up the stairs, Jolene kept close to Winnie. Before entering their room, someone grabbed Jolene's arm. She turned, facing Cora.

"I'm not going to have any trouble with you, am I? 'Cause if I do, I'll break you, hear me? I've come a long way since the plantation. I'm not ever going back; you understand...I said...do you understand?" Cora shouted into Jolene's face.

Jolene just nodded.

"Good! Now, get to bed," Cora said, and then walked away.

Later on, lying in bed, Jolene felt too miserable to sleep.

"Jolene, are you crying?" Winnie called from across the dark room.

"I can't do this, Winnie. I've got to get out of here."

"There's no escaping. What are you thinking? Just do your best, and one day you'll be living high on the hog off of some rich white boy whose daddy has enough money to choke a horse."

"But I'm a virgin."

"That's all the better," Winnie declared. "They pay more for virgins."

"You don't understand. I'm saving myself for the man I'll love."

Winnie laughed so hard she nearly fell out of bed.

"It's just not in the cards, girl. Just get it out of your head."

"You don't understand," Jolene argued, again. "It's more than just that. It's…"

"It's what?" Winnie asked, wanting to know.

"It's a sin. God doesn't approve of such things. It's a sin."

Winnie stopped laughing. "You're kidding me, right?"

"It's a sin," Jolene insisted.

Winnie let out a long sigh. "Turn over and go to sleep, girl. We got a busy day, tomorrow."

****

Weeks passed, slowly turning into months. Surprisingly, it was hard work. There were classes, everyday. They received lessons in grooming, how to walk, how to talk, to be entertaining, always smiling no matter the situation. They were even taught how to read and write, which white society looked down upon, and a crime in certain areas of the South, punishable by fines and prison time. All classes were taken up with the utmost seriousness. One false move or incorrect answer, Cora was on them with a switch, beating their palms bloody.

In the midst of all this, Jolene had only two consolations that kept her going. Every night, in bed, she prayed in the dark. With tear-filled eyes she prayed to God to free her from the path she was on, to guide her and strengthen her, especially to not give into temptation. The only other comfort in her life was Winnie. They became good friends. Though Winnie's philosophy of life differed from hers, Winnie was always sympathetic, always lending a hand or an ear.

One night, at the dinner table, Madam made an announcement that tore through Jolene's heart. Her life collapsed in a moment.

Madam tapped her butter knife on the side of her drinking glass to get the other's attention.

"Ladies, it gives me great pleasure to announce that Winnie has graduated. She's been selected by a very wealthy gentlemen. The arrangements have been made; all the papers have been signed. She will be leaving us in the morning for her new life. I hope all of you will join with me in congratulating her and wishing her well."

Everyone applauded, except Jolene. She leaned over to Winnie.

"Why didn't you tell me?" she whispered, her hands and voice shaking.

"Later…" Winnie spoke softly from the side of her mouth.

Alone in their room that night, Jolene was beside herself in tears.

"What will I do once you're gone?"

"You'll go on living," Winnie demanded. "I don't understand you. Do you want to go back to being a slave working in the fields? You have a chance for the best life possible."

"But at what cost?"

"What are you trying to say, Jolene?"

"I'd sooner lose my life, before losing my soul. This is not God's way."

Winnie took hold of Jolene by her arms. "Listen, this God you're always talking about. I know nothing about it. But, I do believe, even if he does exist, he wouldn't want people to suffer. No one should suffer, especially when they have a way to avoid it."

"Oh, Winnie, I won't be able to live once you're gone. I've got to escape, somehow."

"Girl, you know there's no escaping. The guards will be on you in no time. What are you going to do, jump over the wall?"

"I have tried," Jolene responded.

"What…?" Winnie looked at her as if she'd gone mad.

Jolene explained, "The walls are high. One night, I took one of the chairs from the dining room. I put the chair next to the wall, outside. Standing on the chair, I jumped as high as I could, trying to get hold of the top of the wall. I came within inches of getting hold of the ledge. I could do it, if I had help."

Winnie looked at her with suspicion. "What are you asking, Jolene?"

"If you helped me, I could do it. I could escape."

"Oh, no, oh no," Winnie repeated, shaking her head. "I've got only one more day in this hellhole, with a chance to finally have a good life. I'm not going to throw it all away for some crybaby, religious fanatic."

"Winnie, please, you're my only hope. This is your last night here, my last chance. Once you're gone, no one will help me. I'll be alone."

****

As quietly as they could, Jolene and Winnie stole a chair from the dining room. They needed to be careful; though it was dark it was still early, most of the household would still be awake. And of course, there were always the guards to consider.

Jolene wore the clothes she arrived in. A black girl dressed as a fine lady was sure to attract unwanted attention. Winnie was in her nightgown and barefooted. Once Jolene was over the wall, she would have to sneak back into the house, return the chair, and get back in her bed. In the morning, she would deny knowing anything. It all happened during the night while she slept. She could only hope they'd believer her.

Placing the chair against the wall, both of them stepped onto the seat.

"You ready?" Winnie whispered.

"Wait, not yet," Jolene said.

"What, having second thoughts?"

"No, there's something I want to say."

"Not now. We don't have time for long good-byes. Get over the wall and go."

"I want you to know how much this means to me. I want you to know how much *you* mean to me."

"Fine, now just get over the wall."

"You are the sister I never had. I love you."

In the face of the danger of getting caught, in spite of all that was at risk, regardless of loss, this stopped Winnie. It touched her heart to hear that anyone loved her. She long since believed it impossible.

"I love you, too, girl," Winnie said, turning quite for a moment as the two women hugged good-bye.

"Do you think we'll ever meet again?" Jolene asked through her tears.

"It's a big world," Winnie said. "But how many Fancy Girls can there be in it? Of course, we'll see each other, again. I'll show up when you least expect it, like a bad penny. Now, get over this wall."

Winnie cupped her hands at her knees. Jolene placed her foot in the hand-cradle, holding onto Winnie's shoulders for support.

"You ready?" Winnie said. "On the count of three…one…two…three….push!"

With one quick effort, Winnie lifted as Jolene jumped up, her fingers touching the top ledge of the wall, but was unable to grab it.

"Again…one…two…three."

This time Jolene was able to take hold of the ledge. Winnie never stopped lifting. Little by little, Jolene shimmied up the side of the wall, till finally she was able to bring her leg up to the ledge. Once she was in this position, it was easy to go the rest of the way. Sitting on top of the wall, she hesitated for a moment, taking in a quick breath, she jumped down.

"Are you all right?" Winnie called out.

"I'm fine," Jolene called back.

"Jolene...good luck...."

"Winnie...God bless you."

Winnie took the chair, returning to the house.

Four

Sanctuary

In the dark, it was difficult to know what direction she was going. Many times she got lost, finding herself wandering down streets leading her in circles. She did this for hours. All Jolene knew was to move away from the harbor, which was easy to see from afar. As long as she did this, she was moving north, away from the city.

Little by little, the city of New Orleans was in the distance behind her, as she walked a country road lined with trees and fields. It was getting late. She grew tired and hungry. Why had she not taken food for the journey? Where was that journey's end, she had no idea.

She prayed silently for direction. Immediately, she received an answer. Joyous singing from heavenly voices filled the air. The music became louder as she walked on. When she got to the top of a hill, the mystery was solved. Just a few yards ahead was a small country church. The voices grew louder as she approached. Standing outside, she eyed the wooded structure, in need of a new coat of white paint, with its high steeple encasing a rusted bell.

Listening to the singing coming from within, she recognized the hymns, the style of singing – this was a black church. Inside, she found all of the pews empty. At the front, was a small group of twenty singers, mostly women with three or four men. They faced the back of the church. Standing in front of them with his back to her was the pastor, conducting them, his arms flying about wildly; nudging them on to the bliss beyond anything one would call *Joyful Noise*.

Jolene sat in the back pew, warming to the glow of worship, resting in the light. She was so at ease, sleep took her by surprise.

The next thing she knew, she found herself lying flat on the pew, a strong hand gently shaking her awake.

"Wake up, child," a voice spoke softly.

She opened her eyes to a smiling face.

Jolene jumped to a sitting position.

Jolene apologized, "I'm so sorry. I just came in to rest for a moment. I guess I fell asleep."

"No need, child," said the man in a soothing tone. "I'm Reverend Osborne; this here's my church, the *Home of the Good Shepherd*. What is your name, child, and where ya from?"

Reverend Osborne was a middle-aged black man, as tall as most, as full-bodied as most men. His hair was graying on the sides, thinning on top. His wide smile was a crescent moon lying on its side. The edges of which held up two round cheeks, a cluster of small skin tags on each.

"My name is Jolene; I'm from Lexington, Kentucky."

Reverend Osborne laughed, "Ya sure is a long ways from home, girl. Who owns ya, child?"

"I have no Massa save for the Lord. I'm a runaway."

The smile left his face. "That's serious. Ya know where ya runnin' to?"

"I'm not sure."

He shook his head. "If ya gonna runaway, ya gotta have a place to run to, first."

It was too late for such wisdom. Jolene shrugged her shoulders.

"Well, ya can stay here, till we figure what to do with ya. I live in a few small rooms out back, ya can sleep there."

She followed him through a door beyond the pulpit. It was a two-room apartment, a bedroom and a small kitchen that he also used as an office. Stacks of paper littered the small dining table.

"Ya hungry?" he asked.

Though it was true she was hungry, she wasn't starving. She could go another day or so without food. Not wanting to be more of a burden, she answered, "No, sir, but thank you."

"Ya can sleep in my room," he said, pointing to a door off the kitchen. The door was open; it was a small room with an equally small unmade bed tightly fitted between two close walls. A tiny window behind the bed, its panes so filthy no one could see in or out.

"I couldn't do that," Jolene said. "Where would you sleep?"

"Oh, I'll just sleep on this here comfort chair. Most nights that's where I sleep, anyways."

Jolene was too tired to differ. "Thank you, sir."

"We'll figure what to do with ya, tomorrow. God bless ya, child."

Jolene entered the room, closing the door. She fell facedown on the bed. Before she could say her evening prayers, she fell asleep.

****

Jolene woke the next morning to the aroma of coffee and fried dough in bacon grease.

Reverend Osborne was generous in his sharing, comforting in his manner and his speech.

"I need to go into town for a few things. I won't be back till late. While I'm there, I'll speak with some folks I know who may be able to help ya."

"Oh, really," Jolene excitably responded. "Who is that?"

"I'd rather not say until I speak with them."

"What would you have me do while you're gone?"

"I don't know. Clean up whatever ya think needs cleanin'," he suggested.

With that, he bid her good day, and then left. Jolene knew exactly what she wanted to do. She would clean the day away for her gracious protector and benefactor, this man of God.

First, she straightened up the kitchen and then the bedroom. She swept and washed the floors on her hands and knees. After that, she started on the church. Again, sweeping, and then scrubbing the floor. She took a wet rag to the pews and the molding along the walls. When she finished, it was late afternoon. The sun was already descending in the west. Reverend Osborne would be home soon, she decided to surprise him by cooking supper.

She fed the fire in the kitchen stove, putting on a pot of water. There were some vegetables she cut up and a handful of dry beans, which she put in the pot, along with salt, pepper, and whatever herbs and spices she could find.

As she was setting the table, footsteps echoed in the church. The door to the apartment opened. She turned to greet him, only it wasn't the Reverend.

"What are ya doin' here?" shouted a woman as she entered with a smile on her face that disappeared as soon as she saw Jolene. She was a black woman in her thirties, dressed poorly, yet neat and clean. Attractive, in her own way, it was obvious she must have been pretty at one time, when she was younger, before years of hard work and suffering sucked the marrow of her beauty.

"Who are ya?" the woman bellowed, storming toward Jolene. She held no qualms about showing her disapproval.

"I...I..." Jolene found she couldn't speak; she was so caught off guard and frightened.

At that moment, Revered Osborne walked through the door.

"Mrs. Prescott, I wasn't expecting ya today."

"What is she doin' here?" the woman hollered at the Reverend, all the while pointing at Jolene.

Reverend Osborne entered the room, standing next to Jolene.

"Mrs. Prescott, this is a church, a sanctuary for those in need of salvation and hope. This poor child is an orphan of the storms of this world, hungry and weary with no place to rest her head. We need to show pity and reach out to help her."

"I don't remember ya ever takin' pity on any ugly girls," Mrs. Prescott hissed at him.

"My dear, Mrs. Prescott, it's near suppertime, shouldn't ya be gettin' dinner ready for your husband and children?"

"This isn't the last of it," Mrs. Prescott huffed, storming out of the apartment. Her steps pounded on the wooden floor of the church, and then the church door slammed.

"I'm sorry about all that. It was just a misunderstandin'."

Reverend Osborne's explanation didn't sit well with Jolene. She felt uneasy all through dinner.

"That was very good," he commented, sitting back from the table.

Jolene remained quiet.

"I have some good news for ya," he said, taking a slip of paper from his vest-pocket. "Can ya read?"

"A little..." Jolene answered. Part of her training to be a Fancy was learning to read and write.

He handed her the slip of paper, a name and address written on it.

"Mr. and Mrs. La Pire...French, been here forever. They're very old and extremely wealthy. They're in need of a girl, someone to look after them, cook and clean, ya know. I told them ya were a free colored, looking for work. The pay isn't worth the effort, but ya get room and three meals a day."

Jolene took up the paper, folded it, putting it in her pocket.

"Thank you. It's very kind of you. Now, if you don't mind I'd like to clean up and turn in, so I can go apply first thing in the morning."

"Of course, my dear, I understand."

Jolene quickly cleared the table, and then cleaning the kitchen. In the bedroom, she lay on the bed, still in her clothes. After what happened with Mrs. Prescott, Jolene no longer felt comfortable, knowing there was no lock on the door.

Had she slept an hour or more, Jolene couldn't tell. It was still dark. She jolted awake from the weight of someone on top of her, hands searching.

"Reverend Osborne, what are you doing?" she screamed.

"Shut up, ya sinful girl. Tempting men beyond their endurance, I'm bewitched and it's your fault. The sin is on your head, not mine."

Using all her strength, she struggled to get away, except he was too strong for her.

"Please, stop, you mustn't," she cried over and over, only her pleading seemingly enflamed the fire within him.

She was able to get her hands free. She punched on his shoulders, face, and the sides of his head. It was useless. Her blows didn't faze him in the least. Finally, she brought her fist back as far as it would go. It smashed through the window behind the bed. Glass flew everywhere. Without a thought, she grabbed a shard, stabbing the reverend in his throat. His head soared back, as he screamed out in pain. She was then able to get out from under him. She ran to the door. Looking back, she watched him toss about on the bed, holding his throat with blood soaked hands, a gargling noise coming from his large gullet.

She was afraid. Something needed to be done or he'd bleed to death, but what? In the church was a rope that hung along the far wall. She ran to it, and began to ring the church bell. Vowing to send out an alarm until help came. The peel of the bell exploded across the land for miles. Surely, someone would hear it and come to help.

Finally, she saw from the window, lanterns glowing off in the distance, coming closer every minute. Help was on the way. It was time for her to leave.

She ran out of the church, into the darkness, in the direction she had come, toward the harbor of New Orleans. As she ran, she looked down at her hands. They were covered in blood.

Five

Madam and Monsieur La Pire

Jolene hid in the shadows throughout the night. It was foolish to return to New Orleans, knowing they would be looking for her. Nevertheless, if she could find the address written on the slip of paper Reverend Osborne gave her, she might be safe. Of course, it all depended on if they'd hire her, willing to take her in.

She couldn't help thinking about the night before. Had she killed Reverend Osborne? She prayed she hadn't and that help came in time. She hadn't meant to do it, trying to defend herself. After washing the blood from her hands in a puddle in the street, she took out the slip of paper and read.

Mr. and Mrs. La Pire
501 Napoleon Avenue.

It was early morning; the sun was up. People were moving about, starting their day. Jolene rushed about searching for the address, afraid to ask anyone for help. As the morning grew, she became more frightened, knowing the authorities would be looking for her. Finally, she came onto Napoleon Avenue. She followed the numbers.

It was a two-story building. At first glance, it was exquisite. However, with closer inspection, it was easy to tell it was in ill repair. The façade was in desperate need of a new coat of paint; as well, much of the plaster was cracked or fallen away.

Jolene walked up the seven steps to the front door, pulling the handle, the bell rang. She waited nearly a minute, was just about to ring the bell, again, when the door opened.

Jolene was not tall; however, she towered over this miniature white woman. Her back was hunched. Her face wrinkled to the point it seemed to be crumbling. Dressed in the height of a fashion that was popular fifty years prior, the dress looked worn, in need of repair. Like the building itself, the woman was falling apart. Other than her clothing, she wore another outdated item. Her head was crowned with a *Powdered Wig*, something not popular since the late 1700s. Jolene heard of them, but never saw one, before.

"What is it?" the old woman snapped.

"Reverend Osborne sent me. He told me you're looking for a housekeeper."

"Oh, yes, from the colored church. Are you experienced?"

"I'm a good cook, and I'm not afraid of hard work."

The old women opened the door letting Jolene in. As soon as the woman closed the door, an old man, presumably her husband, entered the hall. He was as short, old, and as ill dressed as his wife. His clothing was dated, and again, a powdered wig.

"This girl is here for the housekeeping job," the old woman announced.

"It doesn't pay much," he said. "Bar that, you will have your own room. You may eat whatever is left of our meals. Will that work for you?"

Jolene nodded.

"Where are your things," he said, noticing Jolene was empty-handed.

"I lost them, sir," she said, knowing this was only a half-truth.

"You will address us as Madam La Pire and Monsieur La Pire, you understand? You may sleep in the attic, there are blankets there. You will start immediately. The kitchen is through that door. I expect breakfast within the hour. If it is to our approval, you may have the job."

"Yes, Madam, thank you, Madam."

Jolene rushed to the kitchen. Within the hour she had a meal on the dining room table. The rest of the morning, she spent cleaning till it was time to prepare a midday meal, more cleaning until supper, finally more cleaning till late that night. There was so much to do; the house was in such disarray. When she finally got to the attic, she was exhausted. Lying on a pile of blankets, she said her nightly prayers. She was grateful to be off of the streets. In just that one day she understood what kind of people she worked for. It was not going to be easy.

****

Aldric and Babette La Pire married at a young age in the city of Paris, France. An arranged marriage between two wealthy families, both Aldric and Babette never needed to work for a living, all their lives.

On a whim, in their early thirties, they moved to America, to New Orleans. This was fine with their families, who were disappointed in them, for their laziness and shameful behavior. An allowance was promised to them, with the stipulation they never return to France.

This allowance, though far from meager, forced Mr. and Mrs. La Pire to live a frugal life. This frugalness grew with intensity, till in their old age it blossomed into full miserism. This was the state of being Jolene was confronted with.

The inside of the home was in worse shape than the outside, as weather cannot compete with the havoc human beings can cause. The walls were cracked, in need of paint. It was so long since anyone cleaned the flues, whenever a fire was lit, the clogged chimneys would spew a cloud of ash and smoke.

The elderly couple frowned on the use of candles, thinking it an unnecessary expense. Nights were spent in darkness.

It was difficult working in the kitchen. As soon as you entered, the smell of rotting food would make your eyes tear. Nothing was thrown out, no matter what its condition. Everything was to be eaten. They would cut around the mold and spoilage.

As for the couple themselves, they seldom bathed. Soap was costly. They wore the same clothing everyday. The beddings were never changed.

The reason for the powdered wigs was simple. In the 1700s, powdered wigs came into vogue in Europe during an epidemic of syphilis. One of the ill effects of the disease is the person looses their hair. Thus, the powdered wig became commonplace. Even after the epidemic, powdered wigs remained in fashion into the early part of the 19th century.

Aldric and Babette La Pire wore powdered wigs for the same reason. They were both bald. Remembering how in their youth wigs were a sign of prestige, as only the wealthy could afford them, they purchased two wigs, one for each of them, and only one.

The downside of this was in the heyday of powdered wigs, people of wealth usually owned more than one wig, alternating them often. As well, they were called *Powdered Wigs* because they were sprinkled daily with scented powder. This kept all foul smells at bay. Mr. and Mrs. La Pire, who would not spend a penny on soap, saw no reason to spend even more on scented powder. There was a hole in the wall outside the attic. Every few days, Jolene would scrape some of the plaster out of the hole. They would powder their wigs with this plaster dust. Aldric and Babette La Pire were like their home that was crumbling around them, in ruin and smelling rank as a sewer.

Jolene was miserable. Being the only servant, she did the work of three. To make matters worse, Mr. and Mrs. La Pire were always cruel in manner and speech. She so wanted to leave, only to where, and above all, how. Still, less than three months later it was bitter unseen fate that changed it all for her.

****

"Jolene, get in here this instant!" Madam La Pire ordered from the parlor.

Stepping out of the kitchen, Jolene was confronted with not only Madam La Pire and Monsieur La Pire, but two constables. They were two young men, officers of the law, dressed in their black uniforms with gold badges on the front of their caps.

"Is this the girl?" asked one of them.

"That's her," Madam La Pire said, pointing at Jolene.

"You're under arrest. Come with us," the other constable said.

"I don't understand. What have I done?" Jolene pleaded.

Madam La Pire stepped forward, shaking her finger under Jolene's nose. "We took you in, when you had no place to go. We gave you a position. We opened up our home and our hearts to you; this is how you repay us?"

"I don't understand."

"Don't play innocent with us, girl," Madam said, and then turning to the constables. "I have a very expensive broach that once belonged to my mother. This girl stole it."

"What are you saying, Madame? I've never stolen anything from you," Jolene cried.

"Then who did? You're the only other person in the house. It wasn't my husband and it certainly wasn't me. It had to be you."

"You're mistaken, Madam," Jolene said. "Perhaps, you misplaced it. You know how you forget things."

"Are you calling my wife a liar?" Monsieur La Pire added.

"No, sir, I'm just saying Madam may have misplaced it. It must be somewhere in the house. Just give me some time to find it, I'll prove my innocence."

Madam La Pire began sobbing. "It's not just the money, even though it was worth a lot of money. It's the sentimental value of it that makes it even more valuable, irreplaceable. It was my mother's." Tears flowed from her eyes, down her cheeks. "To think we tried to help this girl; you see how she repays us."

"What is her name?" asked one of the officers, not interested with what Jolene had to say.

"She told us her name was Jolene," Monsieur La Pire said. "If that's her real name, she might have lied about that, too."

"How long has she worked for you?"

"Not quite three months."

"Tell me how did she come into your employment?"

"She was recommended to us by Reverend Osborne."

"Reverend Osborne...?" the officer asked, sounding surprised.

"Yes, you know, the colored preacher from...oh, what is it...that colored church on the edge of the city."

"I know him," the officer replied. "He was murdered in his bed a few months ago."

"Oh, Lord," Madam cried to heaven, "a murderer under our own roof."

"Take her away, officers," Monsieur said.

Each of the constables took Jolene by the arm. Madam held the door for them. She spit on Jolene, as they left.

They placed her in the back of a carriage, taking her to the station. They booked her, and then placed her in a cell. There were females as well as male prisoners, white and black, in the cell with her. They all laughed at Jolene as she fearfully crouched in the corner, crying and praying.

Six

For God's Sake

"Leave her be," a woman said with concern, sitting down next to Jolene. "She's just a child."

"That's the way I like `em," remarked one of the men.

"You would," said the woman. "You probably couldn't handle a real woman."

The other men laughed at him.

"What's your name, child?" asked the woman. "My name is Dominique."

Dominique was a beautiful white woman, as white as a cloud. Her midnight black wavy hair rested on her shoulders, as dark as her eyebrows floating over her hazel eyes. Still, for all her beauty, there was hardness in her face, somewhat cruel, like someone who'd lived, loved, and lost too many times. The most peculiar thing about her was her style of dress, which was in the manner of a man, wearing pants, boots, and a shirt.

"My name is Jolene."

"Jolene, that's a pretty name," Dominique said. "Tell me, why are you here?"

It had been so long since anyone showed the slightest concern for her that Jolene opened up her life to Dominique like someone recites from a book, telling the complete story, leaving nothing out.

Dominique laughed, "You are a goner, for sure. They will hang you as sure as looking at you."

"But I'm innocent," Jolene insisted.

"No doubt you are. Just one look at you tells me you're telling the truth. I don't see innocent folk often, but I know them when I see one. It don't matter none, though. You're a goner. They'll hang you, like they'll hang me." She laughed all the harder.

Jolene began to sob.

Dominique placed her arms around Jolene. "Now, now, don't cry. I got a soft spot for young pretty colored girls. I won't let anything happen to you. Providence has crossed our paths, so I may save you from the hangman's noose and from yourself."

"Myself?"

"Yes, from yourself. I know a case of too much goodness, when I see it. *Goodness* will get you in prison, it will get you hung. I advise you to turn over a new leaf, give up all thoughts of being good."

"But…but…you're here, as well," Jolene pointed out.

Dominique burst into laughter, once more. "Smart as a whip…I like that. Let me introduce you to these three rouge comrades of mine." She pointed to the three young men standing before them. "This is Dog, this here's Nebo, and this is Peanut. Of course, that's not their real names, however when you're wanted by the law, it is best not to use your real name."

All three were slender young men, filthy from head to toe, their clothes worn and torn. None of them wore shoes. Dog was blonde with slightly crossed eyes. Nebo was a short-haired black man with a crazed look about him. Peanut, a small white lad, was as one would assume from his name, a full-head shorter than the other two.

"Why are you here?" Jolene felt free to ask.

"Because, unlike you dear Jolene, we are criminals. What sort of crimes, you may ask? Theft, mostly, one has to make a living. Other than that there have been other infractions, assault, perjury, drunkenness, adultery…Oh, wait adultery's a sin, not necessarily a crime. I always get those two mixed up." Her three associates laughed, finding this amusing, "Oh, and of course, murder."

Jolene's eyes went wide.

"For this, and many other felonies that I can't recall at the moment, we all will be tried and hung." Her three companions found this also amusing.

Tears began welling up in Jolene's eyes.

"Oh, my pretty, don't cry. I won't let any harm come to you. Lie down in my arms, here near the cell door. I will protect you."

"I don't think I should," Jolene said, shyly.

"Oh, right, there's that goodness I warned you about. Well, have it your own way. However, I promise you we'll be free by morning."

"How can that be?" Jolene asked.

"Dominique is here to save you," she assured Jolene as she lay next to the cell door, crossing her arms, and closing her eyes to sleep.

Jolene did not feel comfortable sleeping close to Dominique. Still, if an escape plan was afoot, she wanted to be a part of it. She found a place on the floor a few feet from

Dominique. The other three did the same. Jolene's mind was racing, making it difficult to sleep, yet in time exhaustion overcame her.

****

It was late in the night. Jolene woke up with a jolt. She could hardly breathe, coughing and choking. She could barely see. All around her was smoke.

A guard cut his way through the smoke to unlock the cell door. "The building's on fire! Save yourselves!" he shouted, opening the door.

Dog was the first prisoner out of the cell, he round-housed the guard, knocking the man down, unconscious. Dog ran off, followed by Nebo and Peanut. Dominique took hold of Jolene by the hand, pulling her out of the cell.

Jolene looked down as she stepped over the guard, out cold on the floor.

"We mustn't leave him," Jolene shouted to Dominique over all the screams of the other prisoners.

"Let him burn," was Dominique's answer as she guided Jolene through the smoke and out of the station.

Outside, the chaos was so extreme, prisoners found no problem running away. Dominique and Jolene ran hand-in-hand down the street. They meet the other three down the road.

"Keep moving! We won't be safe till we're out of this town," Dominique warned.

They all turned, ready to run, except Jolene.

"What's wrong?" Dominique asked.

"You knew there was going to be a fire, didn't you? You arranged for there to be a fire," Jolene questioned Dominique.

"Yes, I did," Dominique said. "I paid for the station to burn. Would it make you feel any better if I told you it was a constable who started the fire? Don't be a fool. Come with us," Dominique declared, turning, running off, followed by the three. In fear, not knowing what else to do, Jolene ran with them. They ran till they were safely out of New Orleans.

****

When New Orleans was out of sight, many miles behind them, they came on a small farmhouse a short distance from the road. It was still in the heart of the night, all was dark, save for the lights coming from the home.

Standing on the porch, Dominique knocked on the door, it opened.

"It's about time," said an old man standing in the doorway. He was a short, white man, with snow-white hair and whiskers. He was thin, save for a round gut hanging over his belt buckle.

"Nice to see you, too, Tucker," Dominique said as she pushed him out of the way, entering, the others followed.

It was a small farmhouse with only two rooms. Everyone found a seat to relax in, excluding Jolene who remained standing, feeling and looking awkward.

"Who's the new girl?" Tucker asked.

"The key we've been looking for," Dominique announced to the bewilderment of the others.

"Y'all want somethin' to eat?" Tucker asked.

"Who needs food," Peanut said, "What I need is a drink."

Tucker picked up a jug sitting next to the fireplace. He pulled the cork out, put it to his lips, taking a long pull from it. Then he handed it to Peanut who nursed on it for a few minutes before passing it on.

Feeling worn-out, Jolene sat down on a footstool by the fireplace.

Dominique only took a few drinks from the jug, however it didn't take long before the others were roaring drunk.

Peanut stood up and swaggered to Jolene. "You know what I'd like, right now?" he said, running his hand over Jolene's head. "Tucker, ya mind if I use your bed?"

"Not at all, mate."

"I'm next," shouted Nebo.

"Count me in," Dog added. "How about ya, Tucker?"

"Oh, I'm too old for such nonsense."

They all laughed.

Wide-eyes terror washed over Jolene.

Dominique walked over to Peanut, placing her hand on his shoulder. "Peanut, now you know you can have your way with anyone at anytime, except for gang members."

""She ain't no gang member," he declared.

"Jolene," Dominique said, "would you like to join our gang?"

"What would I have to do?" Jolene asked.

"The same as what we do, we rob and murder."

"I could never do that," Jolene protested.

"Take her, she's yours," Dominique told Peanut.

He grabbed hold of her, pulling her from the footstool, dragging her to the bedroom. The laughter of the others filled her ears.

"No, please, in the name of God, please don't" Jolene begged.

"God who…who is this God?" Dog shouted in drunken laughter. Such talk seemingly inflamed the men; her pleas aroused them, all the more.

"No, please don't!"

Dominique stopped them at the bedroom doorway, which had no door. "Will you join our gang, now?" she asked coldly.

"Yes, I'll do whatever you ask," Jolene said, shaking in fear.

"Then you're in the gang," Dominique announced for all to hear. "Let her go," she ordered Peanut.

He let her loose. Jolene fell to the floor. The men laughed heartily, as she crawled to a corner of the room where she curled up into a ball, crying herself to sleep.

****

They now had horses and guns. Because of the job intended for her, which remained a mystery, Jolene was not given a gun. As well, she didn't know how to ride a horse, so she rode with Dominique, holding on in the back.

They rode slowly through a thick forest. When they got to a sharp turn in the rode, with a steep slope to one sit, they stopped. Carefully, they rode up the slope, till they were well hidden in the woods with a clear view of the road below, coming and going.

They waited in silence, though not for long. Off in the distance, they could see two horsemen coming up the road.

"Here come the fish. Time to put out the bait," Dominique said, helping Jolene down off the horse. "Go down to the road. I want you to stop them. Tell them you're lost. No man can bypass a beauty in distress."

"What are you going to do?" Jolene asked, looking up at them all.

"We're going to rob them, you stupid girl," Dominique said, laughing down on her.

"I won't help you," Jolene proclaimed.

Dominique stopped laughing. "Listen to me, you righteous little beast. This can go two ways. You can stop them; we rob them of their money, guns, horses, and boots. They spend the rest of the day walking back to town, complaining, with a story they will tell their grandchildren. Or if you refuse to help, we go down shooting at them, killing them. So, what's it going to be?"

Jolene didn't need to think it over; she knew what she needed to do, even if it was against her will and better judgment. "Very well, I'll do it."

They watched as Jolene made her way down the slope to the road. She stood in the center of the lane, with her hands waving above her head.

As they approached, Jolene got a good look at the riders. They were two white men, dressed in the manner of wealthy gentlemen. They saw her, as well.

"Out of the way, girl, we don't have time for trash."

"Please, sirs, I'm desperate," Jolene beseeched them.

They stopped, looking down at her.

"She's not hard on the eyes. Maybe, it would be worth a few minutes to stop," said one of the men, dismounting. The other man did the same.

As they approached Jolene, she whispered to them. "Sirs, listen carefully. There are robbers in the woods ready to ambush you."

Only it was too late, the next moment the gang was out of the woods, surrounding them, aiming their pistols at the men.

"Gentlemen, raise your hands and keep them up," Dominique ordered.

They did as they were told. They quickly were stripped of their purses, guns, and boots. Nebo took hold of the reins of their horses.

"You're not going to leave us out here like this, are you?" one of men asked.

"Well, we can't take you with us," Dominique answered back. "You should make town by nightfall."

One of the men looked at Jolene with anger. "We stopped to help you; this is how you repay us?"

Dominique and the others burst into laughter.

"You lying hypocrite," Dominique said, pointing her pistol under his nose. "I heard you. You had intentions. I should kill both of you."

"You promised to spare them," Jolene cried, reaching out to Dominique.

"Why should I?" Dominique said, pulling back the hammer of the gun. It clicked into place. Both prisoners went wide-eyed and into a rapid sweat.

Looking at Dominique's eyes, Jolene knew she was ready to kill both men. She fell to her knees at the feet of Dominique. "Madam, please, don't do this! I will serve you anyway you want for the rest of my life, just don't to this. I beg you. For God's sake don't!"

"You'll have to forgive her. She does this at the most inopportune time. I apologize," Dominique said jokingly to the men standing before her.

"For God's sake, Madam," Jolene pleaded.

"Listen to her," Dominique continued. "She believes in this...God. Do you believe in God?" she asked the man at the end of her gun.

He didn't answer, just standing there more frightened than any time in his life. Sweat dripped over his forehead and down his face.

"I asked you a question," Dominique insisted. "Do you believe in God?"

You could see the man's mind was racing. He knew he had to make a decision. But what answer would appease this madwoman? Finally, he blurted out, "Yes, I believe in God!"

Dominique smiled. "Well, then you can just go to him." She pulled the trigger. The gunshot was loud as a cannon blast, echoing off the hills. The bullet entered his forehead, creating a small hole, a trickle of blood oozed out. Yet it was the back of his head that was most disturbing. The back of his head exploded, splattering pieces of brains and bone in every direction. The body fell to the ground with a thud.

"No!" Jolene screamed, falling flat to the ground next to the body.

Dominique turned her attention to the other man, aiming her pistol at him. "What about you? Do you want to see your creator?"

"No," the man stuttered.

"Why not...?" Dominique asked. "What's wrong, don't you believe in God?"

The man muddled over the question. He understood the importance of the answer. He looked at the body of his friend lying at his feet. A proclamation of faith had not helped him. He made a decision to try the other path.

"No, I don't," he said.

"Don't what?" Dominique persisted. "I want to hear you say it."

"No...I don't believe in God," he replied.

"Then here's one for Satan," Dominique said, pulling the trigger. The man fell dead atop of his companion.

Jolene wriggled on the ground, as if in pain.

"She's useless," Dominique concluded. "Get rid of her."

Peanut stood over Jolene, slowly unbuttoning the front of his trousers.

"No, none of that," Dominique said. "She's still part of the gang, a useless one, yes, but still one of us."

With that Dog, Nebo, and Peanut stood over her kicking her with all their might. They continued till each one of them had kicked every part of her, till she was bloody from head to toe. When they felt sure she was dead, they mounted their horses, riding off down the road.

Seven

Lose

Jolene had no idea how long she lay on the road, unable to move or even open her eyes. She woke to excruciating pain. Her ribs were cracked: she could taste her own blood in her mouth. It must have been days, she could smell the rotting corpses on the road next to her.

Vultures swooped down upon the corpses to feast. One of beasts sat atop Jolene, pecking at her shoulder. It took all her strength, waving her arms about, scaring away the animal. The pain of movement was so great, she went unconscious.

In her stupor, she felt two strong arms lift her up, carrying her into the woods. She felt the warmth of a fire, water poured gently into her mouth. A cool wet rag washing the blood from her face, cleaning her wounds.

When she woke in the morning, she was able to open her eyes. She was propped up against a log, a fire at her feet. She was alone. Placing her hands on her side, she felt twigs that had been tied to her, keeping her broken ribs in place. It hurt just to breathe.

A man came out of the woods, carrying a bundle of dry logs for the fire.

"Oh, you're awake," he said. "How do you feel?"

"What happened?" she asked.

"I'm sorry to tell you this. I found you and your companions lying in the road. I'm sorry, but their both dead. I buried them in a field over yonder. You were barely breathing when I found you. Whoever it was who killed your friends beat you up pretty bad. They left you for dead."

"How long have I been like this?"

"I don't know how long you've been lying in the road. I brought you here three days ago."

"Who are you?" Jolene asked.

"The name's Graham Dorsey. What's your name?"

"Jolene…Jolene Fairchild."

"Robbers…?"

"How's that…?"

"Robbers, was it robbers who beat you?"

"Yes, it was robbers," Jolene admitted, knowing it was only a half-truth.

"All you've had is water. You need to have something to eat," he said, taking a crust of bread from a sack, handing it to Jolene. Bringing it to her mouth, she bit off a piece. It felt painful to chew.

Graham Dorsey was a young, tall white man, over six feet. He was lean, muscular with raven black hair, and chiseled good-looks. Jolene couldn't recall ever seeing a more handsome man in her life. He was dressed western-style, in black from heat to toe, from his wide-brim hat down to his leather boots.

Jolene knew little if not less to nothing about guns. The six-gun on his hip was clearly no ordinary weapon. Its alabaster handle shown in rainbow colors, the silver glowed, the holster was handcrafted just for that one pistol.

"Graham," Jolene said. "What is it you do?" She knew the question was a personal one, still her curiosity stirred in her.

"Jack of all trades, master of none," he answered. "I guess you could say I'm a *Soldier of Fortune*."

"You mean you're a gunslinger."

He laughed, showing a fine row of white teeth. He was even more handsome when he smiled.

"Yeah, I guess you could say that was a more accurate term to describe what I do." He noticed the conversation was taking too much out of her. "Hey, we can talk later. Close your eyes and get some sleep. The best thing for you now is rest."

"Thank you for this," she murmured as she closed her eyes.

"Don't mention it."

The crackle of the fire was the last thing Jolene heard before she fell asleep, again.

****

As the days passed, Jolene became better. She was able to sit up and move around. The pain became less.

Graham knew his way around a forest. He found a source of water, collected roots and berries, and trapped small animals. He kept his horse close and hobbled. They wanted for nothing.

In Jolene's eyes, Graham was heaven-sent, a saint, an angel of mercy. Excluding her parents, no one ever treated her so well in her entire life. After all she had been through; it was a joy to meet such a fine soul. As well, Graham was so easy on the eyes, it was understandable that strong feelings grew within Jolene's heart where she held a special place reserved for him. It's only a gentle wind needed to sway a young girl.

"In your work, have you ever killed anyone?" Jolene asked one night after supper, sitting together, staring into the fire.

The question took him off guard; Graham smiled, shaking his head. "A farmer grows a crop, the carpenter cuts wood, and a blacksmith bends metal. A man has to do what he has to do."

"Then you have?" Jolene pressed the point.

Realizing she would not let it go, he answered, "Yes, I have. I try to come to a conclusion without killing, if I can. Usually, it's not possible. It is my job, you understand?"

Jolene thought this over a moment. "But what about your soul...? It's a sin."

"Is it?" Graham asked. "The greater sin is a man who doesn't follow his path, no matter where it leads."

"Sometimes that path takes you to places you shouldn't go," Jolene responded. "I want my life to be one of goodness. When I move without goodness, the path walks me, not the other way round, as it was intended. There is no good without God."

Graham looked at her strangely.

"I once killed a man," Jolene confessed. "I didn't intend to; it was an accident, but he's still dead, nonetheless. If I had been walking in goodness, perhaps he'd still be alive."

"I believe in nature," Graham said, "what you can see, feel, and touch. You cannot fight nature. In each of us is a nature that you must follow. Fight it as you may, it will always win in the end."

"I don't believe that," Jolene replied. "I believe love and goodness will overcome in the end. Evil may reign for a time, it may win the battle, but it will never win the war. Love and goodness will always prevail."

"You're a funny girl," Graham whispered, moving closer to her.

Jolene heard nothing except her heartbeat, no crackle of fire, the wind in the trees, just her heart pounding in her chest.

Graham reached across, pressing his lips to hers. The world spun as they kissed. It was soft and gentle, what fairytales are made of.

Like a true gentleman, Graham moved away, lying a few feet from her. He closed his eyes to sleep. Jolene did the same.

As sleep took hold of her, she said a silent prayer, a prayer of thanksgiving. This was the answer to her suffering, striving to maintain true to goodness. The answer was love.

****

The days went by tenderly. There was sweetness in the air. Jolene became better with each passing day. She began moving about, going on short walks with Graham.

"I'm no doctor, however, I'd say you're well enough for us to leave," Graham announced one evening. "Let's get some rest. We can leave in the morning."

"Where will we go?" Jolene asked.

"Anywhere your heart desires," he said, and then kissing her.

They slept close to the fire, in each other's arms as they had grown accustomed to. It was late in the night, Jolene woke. His arms were around her, blanketing her, keeping her warm, protecting her. She lay there, watching him sleep. The dying flames made the shadows dance over his face. He looked so handsome.

"So, this is love?" she whispered to herself.

It went against her better judgment; still, she couldn't help herself. She reached forward, placing her lips on his. She kissed him till he woke; he kissed her back. He lifted himself up, the upper part of his body upon her. Then he moved the rest of himself atop her, his weight covering her, pinning her down. His hands explored her, grabbing a handful of skirt, pulling up the hem, exposing her legs.

"Graham, please," she whispered in his ear. "Please, don't." He didn't stop. She understood how difficult it is for a young man, so she remained calm and tactful. "Please, Graham, we mustn't."

It was as if he wasn't listening, or perhaps he couldn't. Once he crossed over the river of his passion, burning that bridge, there was no turning back.

She squirmed under him, gasping for air.

"Please, Graham, not like this," She implored, her words falling on deaf ears.

She began to fight him, only he was far too strong. Freeing her hands from under him, she pounded her fists on his back. Nothing fazed him, he held only one thought. She screamed, again, without a sound reaching him.

She fought as best she could, till all strength left her. She lay under him, lifeless, like a rag doll. He reached down to undo his trousers.

"No…no…no," she cried, shaking her head from side to side.

She didn't understand how something everyone told her was bliss could hurt so badly. How could an act that the world called *Making Love* have an evil side to it?

When it was over, she lay under him in pain. Physical pain, yes, only there was more to it than that. There was the pain of loss, not in the way one might think, in the loss of faith and trust, the loss of her love for Graham.

He rose, redoing his trousers. His touch sent her into a fit of crying. Her expression of grief was beyond words.

"Stop crying, will you?" he hollered at her. This only made matters worse. She cried louder and harder.

"I said, 'stop crying'!" Then he brought his fist down, crushing the side of her face. "Stop…crying!" he repeated over and over, punching her hard after each word he spoke. She cried all the more. He stood up over her, kicking her.

"Oh, God…" she howled.

"Enough talk about this God of yours," he screamed down at her, kicking her.

For many days, he helped her to heal. He knew all the right places to kick that would produce the most pain.

"I told you I must follow my nature. It is you who goes against your nature. It is unnatural to be the way you are, to think the way you think. You owe me. I did all I could to help you, this is how you repay me?"

Kicking her a few more times, he took up his belongings, mounted his horse, riding off.

As the sound of him galloping away into the night faded, Jolene prayed for the salvation of his depraved lost soul. She vowed to never sway from the path of goodness and righteousness, virtue and morality. She sobbed uncontrollably till sunrise, when in exhaustion, she finally fell fast asleep.

Eight

A Savior is a Savior

It took days for Jolene to heal enough to move around. Even then, all she could do was move slowly, stumbling, sometimes crawling on her hands and knees, to a nearby stream where she was able to a get a drink of water.

There was nothing to eat, Graham had taken everything.

It was nearly a week before she felt well enough to move on, away from the stream, into the forest. Going without food, she was in a constant weakened state.

She wandered about the woods aimlessly for days. Many times she would look down at the ground only to realize she was walking over ground she'd traveled before; she'd been walking in circles.

A few times she pulled up roots for food, not always with good results; often it made her sick to her stomach.

She slept when she could on the ground, covering herself with leaves for warmth, mostly for only a few hours. The days were hot, the nights were cold, both long beyond belief.

It was afternoon when she came upon a small clearing in the woods. She was just about to enter when she felt a fainting spell seize her, brought on by hunger. She fell to her knees in prayer.

"Oh Lord, forgive me for my faults. You are the light to my feet, guide my steps. Look down on me, send down your mercy. I have suffered so; I wait on you day and night. You are my only hope. Have pity on your children..."

Before she could finish her prayer, she was interrupted by the sound of footsteps through leaves across the clearing. After all she'd gone through, Jolene had learned to be cautious, no longer trusting blindly, fearing what might be around the next bend. She went silent, hunkering down to the ground behind a thick bush.

Two young men entered the clearing. They were both in their twenties, white, well-dressed, though one of them wore what was clearly a far superior suit, well tailored with a bunch of lace at his throat.

"This will do," the better dressed young man said to the other, looking about the clearing carefully. One might say he inspected it; for what, Jolene had no idea.

They were both about the same height and weight, tall and slender. Both were very good looking. One was dark haired, a strong face with a thin mustache over his thin lips and thick long sideburns. The other, the better dressed one, was blonde, fair skinned and clean shaven. His eyes were richly blue like two robin's eggs sitting on fine chinaware. His lips were small for a man, as red as glowing coals. There was a striking quality about his face. It was the sort of face one expects to be worn by a stage actor, a blank slate that anything could be written on. He moved about like royalty, proud and majestic. His actions dictated he was the leader of the two, dominating their every move.

"Come to me, James," said the blonde gentleman.

To Jolene's surprise, the two men fell into each other's arms, kissing. It struck Jolene as being an illusion, like watching a man kissing his own image in a mirror, only one was dark, the other light. She never knew such things existed. She was amazed and confused, all at once.

The blonde young man pressed his companion against a tree, unbuttoning the front of his shirt, reaching his hand within, caressing his chest. Never once did they stop kissing, as they embraced.

Jolene reached up to get a better look. In doing so, a twig under her foot snapped.

Instantly, the blonde young man backed away from his partner. "Did you hear that?"

"Hear what?" said James. "I didn't hear anything."

"I'm sure I heard something."

"Don't be so worried, Karl. There's no one here but us. Now, come back to me," James implored.

"No, I heard something."

Karl walked around the clearing, staring into the woods. Jolene held her breath, trying not to make a sound. When he got to where she was hiding, he stood listening. It would seem she'd go undetected.

"What are you doing there, girl," Karl shouted, suddenly grabbing hold of Jolene, pulling her into the clearing. "See, I told you I heard someone," Karl called over his shoulder to James.

He dragged her toward James. There was a tall thin birch tree. He pressed Jolene hard against it. Using his handkerchief, he tied her arms behind it. James came over, standing alongside Karl.

"Who are you, and what did you see?" Karl demanded.

James opened up a small jackknife, pressing it to her throat. "Answer him," James said firmly.

Jolene's thoughts raced through her brain. For some reason, something Dominique once told her came to mind. "When you're wanted by the law, it is best not to use your real name." Jolene was wanted by the law for theft and murder.

"Fancy...they call me Fancy."

Both Karl and James smirked at this.

"What did you see?" Karl barked.

"I saw nothing, sir."

James pressed the knife till it pierced her skin. A thin line of blood flowed down her front. "Answer him," James growled.

"I...I...I saw you two kissing."

"What were you doing hiding? Who sent you?" Karl asked.

"No one sent me. I came upon you by accident. I've been lost, wandering the forest for days."

Jolene's appearance gave weight to her answer. She looked hungry, tired, filthy, and unkempt.

"Please, sirs, have mercy on me," she implored "I have gone through so much suffering, all undeserved."

"Undeserved!" Karl laughed. "No one is clean in this world. All have sinned, no matter how small the infraction. We are all no better than beasts."

"True, sir, but there is an escape, there is forgiveness, and finally redemption."

"You speak like a Christian," Karl remarked.

"Yes, I am, sir. I am a child of God."

"Oh, you're one of those," Karl snorted. "Well, let me tell you I've never had use for this god that you and everyone speak of, and even less care for his children. I want nothing to do with this Shepherd or his sheep."

Karl guided James' hand from her throat; he folded his jackknife, putting it back in his pocket.

"Don't worry," Karl continued. "We won't molest you. You are not the right gender, or the right color, if truth be told."

James laughed, finding it all amusing.

"Nor will we give you charity. We could kill you right here and now without as much as an eye blink. However, I'm feeling benevolent, today. I will show you mercy."

With that, Karl reached around, untying Jolene. He pointed beyond the clearing to the north.

"Past these trees, less than a quarter mile, is the *Lange Estate*, where I live with my grandmother. We have only two coloreds who live and work there; one is a cook who looks after the house. As well, we have a man who looks after the horses and the grounds. You, my dear child, will be Grandmother's servant. Lord, knows how old she really is. The old girl needs someone to look after her, certainly not me."

The two men took hold of her, guiding her through the woods. As Karl said, in less than a quarter mile, they cleared the forest. The first thing she saw was a large two-story home in the fashion of many southern mansions. It was grand in size and design. A few yards from the main house stood a large barn. Nothing else was on the property. There was a saddled stallion tied to a post in front of the house.

"Dear, James, I'm sorry the way this day turned out. I will make it up to you," Karl whispered.

"Think nothing of it," James replied, as he mounted his horse.

The two reached out to each other taking the other's hand, their fingers intertwined.

"I will send word when I'm free to return. Stay well, my dearest Karl."

In an instant, James galloped away. Karl stood watching till James was out of sight over the ridge.

"Come, girl," Karl said, pulling her up onto the porch, and then into the house.

He dragged her from room to room till they got to the kitchen. There they found an old black woman before the stove, standing at a table, cutting onions.

"Nanna, this is the new girl," Karl said, pushing Jolene toward the woman.

Nanna stopped cutting, looking Jolene up and down. "Kind of scrawny, "she remarked.

"She will be taking care of my grandmother, directly. I need you to clean her up before I present her."

"Like I don't have enough to do, today," Nanna complained.

"I know I can always depend on you," Karl said with a snicker. As he was about to leave the kitchen, he had one last thought. "By the way, what's for supper?"

"Your favorite...sauerbraten with potatoes and greens..."

"Ah, just like mother used to make," Karl laughed.

"Your mother never cooked a day in her life," Nanna said sarcastically.

"Don't I know it," he smirked. "May she rest in peace," he said as he turned and left.

Taking two wooden buckets each, Nanna and Jolene went to a well at the back of the house. They drew all four buckets. Nanna handed Jolene a piece of soap and a towel

"What's your name, girl?"

"Fancy."

Nanna made a face indicating she didn't believe it a legitimate name, still, she shrugged it off, believing people could call themselves anything they wanted.

"Nanna, how long have you been here?"

"A lifetime, I've cooked here for two generations."

"What's it like here?" Jolene asked, sounding worried.

"Oh, it's better than most, though it can get strange, at times."

"Strange, what do you mean?"

"You've seen Master Karl. You see what he's like. He's not fooling anybody. Some folks say he..."

Nanna stopped midsentence, catching herself, as if she had gone to the boundaries set for her, not wanting to cross that line, for fear of...?

"What about his grandmother?" Jolene asked.

"Mrs. Lange...she's a saint."

****

The upstairs bedroom was large, dark, and stuffy. The old woman sat in an armchair by a window, dozing.

"Wake up, Grandma," Karl said, gently shaking her shoulder. The old woman's eyes opened. She smiled when she saw his face. "Wake up, Grandma. I've got a present for you. This is Fancy; she's come to take care of you."

"Karl, how handsome you are," she said.

"This is Fancy, she's going to take care of you," he repeated.

She was a frail old soul. Even seated you could tell she wasn't very tall, that her body was petite. She looked like a tiny sparrow sprawled in the chair. Her hair sat upon her head like snow covers a mountaintop on high, an eagle's nest made up of white twigs and straw. Her dress was plain, simple with a crocheted yoke across her chest.

The moment her eyes met Jolene's, a large smile appeared on her face, beaming back at the girl.

It amazed Jolene, touching her heart. Never in her life, except for family and friends, had anyone ever smiled at her before there was a word spoken. Strangers don't simply smile at strangers.

"A present for me?" the old woman questioned what her grandson stated when he woke her. "It's a young girl," she commented. "You can't make a present of a person to another person, a surprise, but not a present. Presents are wrapped in fine paper with ribbons and bows. Things like hard candy and family photographs, yes, but not people."

Karl let out a long sigh, as if he had heard it all and too many times. He rolled is eyes, clearly tired of her. They were oil and water in the same container, together yet separate.

Karl looked to Jolene.

"You're to help Nanna in the kitchen, also with cleaning the house whenever my grandmother is asleep. When she's awake, I want you by her side. Help her in anyway she asks. Get whatever she needs. See that's she's fed and cared for; everyday. Do you understand?

Jolene nodded.

"Good. Can you read?"

"A little," Jolene answered.

"Good, she likes to be read to. There are her books over there. Well, I'll leave you to it." He pulled Jolene to the side, not that it made any difference to the old woman who was oblivious to her surroundings, and whispered. "I'm letting you live to serve my purposes. If you ever displease me, you won't know what happened. You'll just be dead."

Karl turned and left the room, closing the door behind him.

"Mrs. Lange, is there anything you need?" Jolene asked.

"Sit down, child; talk to me," the woman smiled up at her.

Jolene pulled a chair to the window next to her. She sat down. Looking out, she saw the forest she came from and spent so much time in.

"What is your name?" the old woman asked.

"My name is Fancy."

The old woman chuckled. "That's a strange name. It doesn't sound German."

"It isn't German, it's American."

"You don't look German."

"I'm not German, Ma'am, I'm colored."

Mrs. Lange reached out, taking hold of Jolene's hand. She held it to the light coming through the window. She examined it for a moment. "Really, what color are you?"

"No, Ma'am, I mean I'm black."

Mrs. Lange took a closer look at Jolene's hand, "I wouldn't say that. Actually, you look brown to me."

Jolene just smiled; knowing to take the conversation any further would be futile.

"Jesus was a brown man, did you know that?"

"No, I didn't know that," Jolene replied.

"It's true," Mrs. Lange said, pointing across the room. "It's in the Good Book. Go over there and get my Bible. I'll show you."

Jolene went to the far wall where there was a four-row bookcase. She found the Bible. Bringing it back, she sat down again with the book in her lap.

"Now, open to the book of Revelation, chapter one, verses fourteen through fifteen."

Jolene opened the book, thumbing through the pages randomly, clearly in deep waters.

"I'm sorry, Mrs. Lange, I don't know how to…"

"That's all right, child," the old woman smiled kindly, reaching for the book. She flipped through the pages till she got to the correct verses. "Now, read that section."

Jolene read aloud, slowly, pronouncing ever word clearly. "*His head and his hair were white like wool; and his eyes were like a flame of fire. His feet were like fine brass, as if burned in a furnace; and his voice the sound of many waters.*"

"See, I told you the Bible described Our Lord as being brown. Brass is brown, Jesus is brown. Just like you." The old woman laughed out loud. "To be honest, I could care less if he were purple. A savior is a savior."

Jolene smiled, thinking perhaps there are many saviors in one's life, and maybe Mrs. Lange was one of them.

Nine

Story of Four

Newlyweds Karl and Nadine Lange were young and in love. At the turn of the 18th century all talk was of how easy it was to make a good living, if not to become wealthy, in America. Except, it takes a fair amount of money to go sailing across the ocean and have money enough to survive once you arrive.

For Karl and Nadine, being from a small farming village in central Germany, this was a dream well out of reach.

Word among young workingmen was there was work to be found in Bremerhaven, a city on the sea. A handful of investors put their money into the city with hopes of turning it a major seaport. It was a good opportunity for a young man who saw nothing in his future other than dirt farming to move to Bremerhaven, get in on the bottom floor with hopes of a better future. It was a gamble, one that Karl and Nadine were willing to take.

After three short years, through hard work, scrimping and saving, the couple could afford a one-way ticket on a ship sailing for America. The plan was for Nadine to return to their little village, live with her parents, while Karl sailed for America to seek his fortune. Once he was established, he would send for Nadine.

As everyone knows, plans are the cosmic joke of the universe played on mankind. Once in America, Karl traveled about the country looking for work, never finding his niche. He spent time as a laborer, a mule skinner, a lumberjack, and picking crops alongside black slaves in the south.

So much time passed, if not for his monthly letters, Nadine would have feared him dead.

Arriving in New Orleans, Karl tried his luck as a hand on a fishing boat. He finally found his role in life. He seemed an expert from the start. In a year's time, he was able to buy his own boat with his own crew. It was then, after three years of waiting, he sent for Nadine.

They settled in New Orleans. It was there they had their first and only child, Stefan, a handsome boy with his mother's good looks and his father's fortitude.

Being a man of vision, Karl was clever to see beyond his fishing business. Every spare dollar he was able to save, he invested in small businesses. After twenty years, the Lange family was one of the wealthiest in the county.

When Stefan was a young man, he met and fell in love with Christina Agno, a slender beauty from a family of wealth. They married, settling in a part of town that was near both families. After two years of praying and hoping, they had a child, a boy they named Karl to honor Stefan's father.

After many more years of working and investing, Karl senior decided it was time for retirement. He split his dynasty in half, giving his son one half to run as he saw fit. The other half Karl senior sold at a high profit. Banking most of the money, he purchased property north of New Orleans, a four-hour horse ride away. There, sparing no expense, he erected a two-story mansion. He intended that Nadine and he would live out their final golden years in luxury.

Again, fortune laughed, once the building was up and they moved in, Karl died in his sleep. His heart simply gave out.

It was intended, Nadine would return to New Orleans to live. There she would be near her son and family, and of course, her grandson, Karl junior, who was now in his late teens.

Again, it was not to be, sorrow plagued the Lange family. Both Stefan and Christina were killed in a freak accident. One Sunday on their way to church, their buggy slipped down a ravine on the side of the road, rolling over on them. Thankfully, their son, Karl junior, was not with them, but away at school.

Heartbroken, Nadine decided to continue living in the mansion intended for Karl and her. She was already an old woman, still she felt up to Karl junior moving in with her. Perhaps, they could be a comfort to each other.

Never again, would anyone call her by her name, Nadine. With Karl senior gone, from then on she'd only be called *Grandma* or *Mrs. Lange*.

****

Karl junior was a lovely child, the joy of his grandparents. It was his parents, Stefan and Christina who found him a burden. This was a fact, not just a feeling of young Karl. Many times, late at night, he overheard his parents stating this fact.

Unable to show true concern and love for their son, they showered him with material wealth. There was nothing he might desire they didn't make flesh. In a very short time, still a child, young Karl was spoiled, mistrusting, distant, and cold to the world. If not for the times in his life when he was in contact with his loving grandparents, the boy would have turned out to be an uncivilized beast.

As soon as he was old enough to comprehend, his parents sent him off to boarding school. He would remain there even during the summers, only returning home for holidays. Even then, often, spending these times with his grandparents, as his parents often would travel abroad during the holidays, never considering taking their son with them.

As for life at school, the boy was known as a good student, smart, with a quick grasp of every subject. Not often to cause disturbances or infractions of rules, he was well-behaved. Still, there were noticeable parts of his character that concerned school staff, the headmaster and board. Alone, the boy was always melancholy to a fearful point. Around others he was friendly to a fault, so much so, it was clear it was a façade, a show to disguise his true feelings and intent.

As well, the boy was a manipulator, often getting weaker boys to do his bidding. He could talk the devil out of his pitchfork, and he knew it, using it to his advantage whenever possible.

There was another facet to young Karl that was and remains a secret to all save a chosen few. It is a well established fact that young men in boarding school, sealed off from the rest of the world, especially the company of young women, that some will experiment with matters of intimacy. For most, it is nothing but a passing phase, forgotten and buried in the memory. Except for young Karl, it became a way of life. This was who he was. Any alternative held no interest for him.

There is a rumor spoken in certain circles of New Olean's society. When Karl's parents were killed in an accident, word was sent to him about the incident. Only he was nowhere to be found. They searched the entire campus with no sign of him. Then, as if by magic, twenty-four hours later, they found him in his room, asleep. It was surmised that he'd learned about his parent's death from some unknown source. Stricken by shock of such a loss; the poor boy went into hiding to grieve. Others, however, believed young Karl had a hand in their deaths. He was nowhere to be found for twenty-four hours because he was in New Orleans to kill his parents. This, of course, is all speculation, and even if it was true, there would be no way to prove it.

While Karl senior was still alive, in the event of the death of Stefan and Christina Lange, according to wills drawn up, all assets would become the property of Nadine Lange. Nothing would go to Karl junior. Although, it stated that at the death of his grandmother, all of the Lange property and funds would be his inheritance.

After the funeral, his grandmother immediately sent word to the school that Karl junior would see out the term and then leave to live with her. Under her care she would see to his education and well-being. He was her only family, now, she was determined he would never want for anything.

****

Willamina Brown showed promise early on in her life as a cook. She had a knack for southern cooking, and in time international fare. At the age of sixteen, she was the head of the kitchen in the main house of a large plantation.

As the years went by and she became more experienced at her craft, she became a high-priced commodity. Whenever an owner needed money, she was sold. As her expertise grew so did her price. She was sold many times till there were times she didn't even know who owned her, not that it mattered, a kitchen is a kitchen.

Finally, she wound up in the Lange mansion. That was where she was christened Nanna, a European title of affection. By then she was old and in less demand, which was for the best. She was tired of moving around, Mr. and Mrs. Lange were good people and treated her well. When Mr. Lange died, his wife was all she had to cook for, that is until the grandson moved in.

It was an easy life. Mrs. Lange treated her as if she were family. As for the grandson, Karl, she had his number. She'd caught him many times with a friend in intimate moments. She never said a word about it to anyone. As long as she stayed mum, Karl was her friend, or at least not an enemy, and God help anyone who was.

****

There is one last person who lived and worked on the Lange Estate that has not been mentioned as of yet. He was William Cook, everyone knew him as Billy.

Billy was a young black man, no more than two years older than Jolene. He was average in built and in height. What made him unique was his manner, a calm, friendly demeanor. Everyone warmed to Billy. However, it wasn't just people he had this effect on. It was the same with animals. Dogs, cats followed him wherever he went. Squirrels would not run when he came close, staring at him without fear. It was the same with birds, snakes, and cattle. Most striking was his connection with horses. From an early age, Billy was known for his way with horses. To ranchers, he was worth his weight in gold.

Mr. Lange, who was proud of his horses and enjoyed riding the countryside everyday for hours, bought Billy at great expense. Nevertheless, he always felt the purchase was well worth it.

When Mr. Lange passed on, Mrs. Lange sold most of the horses, only keeping what was needed for her carriage and her grandson's two favorite horses. She kept Billy mostly because she liked him. It was good to have a man about the house that could do the heavy labor, chopping wood, lifting, mending fences, and the like. Mrs. Lange could not depend on her grandson, Karl, for such things. He was not one for getting his hands dirty.

There is one last thing that needs to be told about Billy. Something very important, something no one knew or noticed…his deepest secret.

The moment he first set his eyes on Jolene, he was madly and deeply in love with her. Being a shy lad, he kept it hidden within, causing sleepless nights.

Now, knowing all this about the four people that Jolene had to live and contended with, we can continue.

Ten

I Am He

Life was good for Jolene. Nanna was set in her ways, seldom asking her for help in the kitchen or with housework.

There was also a young man named Billy who worked on the property and took care of the animals. He was seldom in the house, except to bring in armfuls of wood for the stove and fireplaces. Billy was such a shy lad, especially around women, he and Jolene rarely exchanged more than pleasantries.

Most of Jolene's time was spent looking after Mrs. Lange. The old woman was no bother, requiring little. Her days she slept away in a chair near the window. Jolene would bring her meals three times a day. Read to her in the afternoons and at night. Lastly in the late evening, Jolene would bring Mrs. Lange a cup of warm cocoa, and then tuck her in bed for the night. It was a joy being with Mrs. Lange; Jolene cherished her time with the old woman, and in time a strong respect and love bonded the two.

Still, it was no paradise, in many ways it was more a prison, from which Jolene saw no escape. Like all good prisons, there was a warden, Karl. He was there whenever and wherever Jolene turned. He was always abusive both in word and deed. Not a day went by when he didn't beat her for the shear pleasure of doing so. There were even times his partner in such crimes was his beloved James. They would take turns holding her down while the other tortured her. Her only solace was they never took pleasure in her as a woman, though they had their way of degrading her in such matters.

At night, Nanna would retire to her small room off the kitchen. Billy slept in a small corner of the barn. For Jolene, Karl would take her to a small garden shed out back. The tools had been removed. No mattress, not even a blanket was she given. The dirt ground was her bed, which was hot in the summer, cold in the winter, sometimes freezing. Save for this, the height of this derogation was that every night Karl would lock her in, bolting the door.

For the slightest infraction, or for no reason at all, Karl would keep Jolene locked in the shed for days, sitting there in the dark, no food or water. She would remain prisoner till she was inches from death. Only then would he release her. It would take days to recover.

"Where is my Fancy?" Mrs. Lange would ask, as this was her pet name for Jolene.

"Oh, Grandmamma," Karl answered. "The poor girl has been working so hard, I decided to give her some time off. She's on vacation."

"Vacation…? Where…?"

"Oh, I sent her to…," he would think of an answer. "I sent her to Paris, France," he said, finally.

"Oh, Paris is nice. I like Paris. That's so nice of you to do that for her, Karl. You're such a good boy."

The poor woman would believe anything her grandson told her, thinking there was no such thing as monsters in the world, lest of all her beloved Karl.

Jolene never spoke of her mistreatment to Mrs. Lange. What good would it do? If Karl ever discovered there would be hell to pay. Nor did she ever mention it to Nanna or Billy, not wanting to get them involved, though she suspected they knew. But their hands were tied.

There were times during her imprisonment in the shed she'd cry for hours in her misery. Still, never giving up hope, she passed the hours in prayer.

One night when her thirst and hunger seemed too great to bear, her prayers were answered.

She heard someone move about on the other side of the door.

"Who's there?" she called out.

There was no answer. She looked down to the lower edge of the door. There was a clearance of only a couple of inches. A slice of bread and a saucer of milk were pushed under the door to her.

"Who are you?" she asked. There was no answer. "Whoever you are, God bless you."

She heard them walk away.

Though Jolene was grateful, she wondered who her secret benefactor was. This went on for several nights, every night bread and milk were slipped under the door to her. No matter how she pleaded, they never revealed their identity.

One night as the slice of bread appeared at the foot of the door, Jolene reached under the door, grabbing hold of a finger. She pulled till the finger was exposed. It was the hand of a black man, a young man.

"Billy, is that you?"

There was no answer.

"I know it's you, Billy, answer me."

"I can't stand to see ya treated this way," he whispered through the door.

"You mustn't do this anymore, Billy. If you're caught, he'll kill you."

"I don't care," Billy said. "Fancy…?"

"Yes, Billy."

"Fancy, I love ya"

There was a long silence. Billy waited to hear that precious response *I love you, too,* only it never came.

"God sees everything, Billy. He knows your heart. He will reward you tenfold. But you must never do this again. I don't want you risking your life for me."

This was not what he wanted to hear, his heart sank, and still he was determined to win her love.

"I don't do this for God, I'm doin' it for ya."

"Please, Billy, don't do this, for me, please."

"Nothing will stop me, not ya, not Massa Karl, not even God. I love ya, Fancy."

With that he left.

True to his word, he returned every night with his gift of bread and milk. No matter how she pleaded with him, he would never ever speak to her.

Against her better judgment, she reached under the door, touching his hand, in gratitude. She did not want to lead him on, yet she wanted to show her appreciation. For she loved his soul, she loved him like a brother, which would have killed him to hear her say such a thing.

Days later when Karl checked on her, she made believe she was in a faint, though actually she was close to being so. He released her. She struggled to the kitchen, where she would clean up and get something to eat. It would be days before she was well enough to resume her duties.

"So, Fancy, how was Paris?" Mrs. Lange would ask.

Jolene would look at her, befuddled.

"Your vacation, my child, how was your vacation?"

"Oh that…it was just fine. I missed you."

****

After a year, nothing changed for Jolene. Always under the watchful eyes of Karl, she saw no way to escape. If there was one, where would she go? She was still wanted by the law. Slavery is bad, yet still better than the hangman's noose.

Her only joy was her time spent with Mrs. Lange, which is what made this next factor so painful for her.

Jolene was called to the library where Karl waited for her. He sat in a large armchair, sipping brandy.

"Sit down, my dear; we need to have a long talk."

Jolene looked at the arm chair across from him, too afraid to sit down.

"Go ahead, take a seat," he said, calmly, sounding friendly.

Jolene sat down, clearly uncomfortable.

"Brandy?" he said, holding his snifter of brandy up to her.

"No, thank you, sir…"

"I thought not," he said smiling. "Fancy, if that is your name, I doubt it. Fancy, I know we've had our little differences in the past. But now I want that all to change, to turn the page, so to speak. You and I shall bond in friendship. A friendship based on mutual advancement. I believe it's safe to say you're not happy here at the Lange Estate."

Jolene didn't answer. She was too afraid.

"Well, I'll just take that as a yes." Karl took another sip of brandy before continuing. "I've lived here with my grandmother nearly all my life. For the most part, it's been just fine. The Lange fortune is in her name, which was always just fine with me, since I always got what I wanted. Although, lately what I want has been slipping out of my reach. I need more money. I am my grandmother's sole heir. I knew she was old and that it would not be long before she died and left me everything. Yet, I had no idea she would live this long. So, I suggest we give nature a hand."

Jolene stared at him, blankly.

"I'll be blunt," he carried on. "I want the old girl dead, and I want you to kill her for me."

"But, sir, I'm not a murderer."

"Neither am I, but we can learn," he joked. "It would be to both our advantages. I would be wealthy, and you will have your freedom. Once she's dead, I will write up a document stating I relinquish my ownership of you; you'll be a free woman. I will also send you off a rich woman. I will give you one thousand dollars in gold. You see, Fancy, this is for both our benefits."

Jolene remained silent. Karl finished his brandy, and then poured another. On the table, next to the brandy, was a small vile. After taking a sip of brandy, he took up the vile, handing it to Jolene.

"This is poison, very powerful, difficult to trace. Each night when you bring my grandmother her warm cocoa, I want you to put a small drop into her drink. It will take a couple of weeks to overcome her, with such small doses it will be even more difficult to trace. It will look like the old girl died in her sleep. No one will be the wiser."

Jolene looked at the vile, realizing it was time to speak. "I can't do this."

"And why not…?"

"It's against God."

Karl laughed at this. "So, what is your point? If I ever believed there was a god, I would be against him. Let me make my point. Just for argument's sake, let's assume there really is a god. This is the same god who says we have a free will to do whatever we want. Then he lays down laws, condemning us, even punishing us eternally for acting upon that free will. He creates nature, and then goes against it. And may I continue?"

"No, he is a God of love!" Jolene protested.

He took another sip of brandy, first.

"Is he?" Karl questioned with deep sarcasm. "This is the same god who gave you black skin, and then placed you in a society who abhors you. You were born a slave, you will live as a slave, and you will die a slave. Is this the love and mercy you speak about? He's a hypocrite, a liar, and a tyrant. I can offer you far more than he. I offer you freedom and wealth."

He took another drink.

Jolene spoke through her tears. "I love Mrs. Lange."

"And so do I," Karl commented to her surprise. "I adore the old girl. If it wasn't for her, who knows how bad my life would have been. Nevertheless, there comes a time when one is just marking time. She is useless to herself and to the world."

"Not in the eyes of God," Jolene insisted.

"There you go with that god-talk, again. Very well, let me put it to you this way. Either you do as I say or I'll kill you. A slave girl buried in the woods is of no consequence to anyone. I will not take 'no' for an answer."

Jolene believed him. She saw no use in arguing further. The only thing she could do was agree to his wishes. She would not poison her dear friend. If she pretended to, it would give her time. What she needed was time. Perhaps, in time she would think of a way to avoid this tragedy.

"Very well, I'll do your bidding."

"That's a smart girl," Karl remarked, finishing his drink.

"Only, let her blood be on your head."

"Whatever…if that makes you feel better. You can give her the first dose, tonight. Just don't keep the poison in the house. Hide it in your shed, locked away safe, just like you."

Jolene pocketed the vile in her apron, and then stood up to leave.

"Did I say you could go?" he shouted. Jolene turned to stone. "You are dismissed when I say you are."

Jolene stood before him, crying.

"Stop your crying. It makes me sick."

He stood up to address her. From his breath and the way he staggered and mumbled it was obvious he was drunk.

"So, you want to believe in god, do you? I have the power over life and death!" He threw his arms out wide. "Here, behold! I am he. I am your god!"

Eleven

The Final Night

Time passed slowly for Jolene. Each day was tedious torture. Karl was usually nowhere to be found, still she felt like he was watching from afar. She only saw him late at night when he locked her up in the shed.

"All is going as planned?" he would say as she entered, more of a statement than a question.

"Yes, sir," she answered, trying not to look him in the eye, afraid something might give her away. Because, in truth, she never put the poison in Mrs. Lange's evening drink. She would pour a drop or two out the window of the kitchen when Nanna wasn't looking. Seeing the contents lessening with each passing day, made Karl believe all was going as planned. Again, Jolene was only playing for time in hopes something would happen to change it all, only it would have to be a miracle.

She went about her daily chores in silence, rarely saying a word to Nanna. Knowing Billy's feelings for her, she did her best to avoid him. She had her own share of troubles; a young man's crush was not something she wanted to deal with at the moment. Everyone, including Mrs. Lange, sensed something was bothering the young woman, deeply.

"Fancy, what is wrong, my child?" the old woman asked, clearly concerned.

"Why, there's nothing wrong, ma'am."

"Oh, don't try to kid an old kidder," she laughed. "Is it a matter of love? I used to be young once, you know. I know what that's like. You mustn't let that bother you, time heals all wounds."

"I wish it was something that simple," Jolene answered.

"Well then, what has you so down, child?"

Jolene placed the late night cup of cocoa on the windowsill, the window where Mrs. Lange sat. Jolene fell to her knees, placing her hands in prayer upon the old women's knees.

"Mrs. Lange, I have a confession to make."

The old woman said not a word, staring at Jolene, silently listening closely.

"My name's not Fancy; it's Jolene…Jolene Fairchild. I didn't want to use my real name because I'm wanted by the law. I'm wanted for theft and murder."

Mrs. Lange expressed amusement, "That's impossible. You couldn't hurt anyone."

"That's true, madam. It is all a misunderstanding. Nonetheless, I am wanted by the law."

The smile left Mrs. Lange's face.

"There is more," Jolene admitted. "Your grandson, Karl, wants you dead, so he can inherit the estate. He's tried to make me a part of his plan, which is to put poison in your drink every night."

"And have you?" Mrs. Lange asked.

"No, I haven't. Your grandson thinks so, but I haven't. I swear," Jolene said, taking the cup off the windowsill, handing it to Mrs. Lange.

"Fancy, go to the bookshelf. Bring me the Bible."

"But, madam…"

"Just bring it here."

Not understanding, yet not wanting to argue, Jolene fetched the Bible.

"Now, read Mark, go to chapter sixteen, read verse eighteen."

During her time spent with Mrs. Lange; Jolene learned her way through the Bible. She opened to the book, chapter, verse, and read. "*They shall take up serpents: and if they drink any deadly thing, it will not hurt them: they shall lay hands on the sick, and they shall recover.*"

"You see, Fancy, there is no poison that can harm me," Mrs. Lange said as she took a sip from her cup. "You see."

"Because I haven't put any poison in your drink," Jolene insisted. "Your grandson wants you dead."

"That is another thing, young lady. I don't like you bad-mouthing my grandson. He took you in when you needed a place to go. He gave you a good paying job, a nice room for you to sleep in, plenty of good food. He even sent you on holiday to Paris, and this is the way you show your gratitude?"

Jolene realized she would never get the woman to believe her. Mrs. Lange would never be her ally. It was all pointless. All it did was cause the old women to become overly upset.

"I'm sorry, madam, I was only fooling," Jolene said.

"So, it was a joke," Mrs. Lange said, "Well I don't think it's very funny."

"You're right; it was in bad taste, I'm sorry."

Mrs. Lange finished drinking her cocoa, handing the cup to Jolene.

"I'm sorry, Mrs. Lange, it will never happen again."

"What won't happen again?"

As quickly as it started, the incident was over, forgotten. Mrs. Lange's memory was only good with the long-ago, the here and now was often fleeting.

****

It was nearly two weeks later. Mrs. Lange was showing no signs of being ill. Jolene knew Karl was watching. She would have to account for herself, soon.

Each night, Jolene would prepare Mrs. Lange's evening drink, and then bring it up to her room. This night was no different. Nanna had finished for the day and was in her room. Jolene was in the kitchen, alone. The kettle was on the stove. While waiting for the water to boil, she heard someone call her name from somewhere in the house.

"Fancy," the voice called. It was a male's voice. It didn't sound like Karl or Billy. She moved about the house, yet found no one. Perhaps, she was mistaken.

Returning to the kitchen, the kettle was on the boil. She prepared the drink in the usual way, one part boiling water, one cocoa, one part milk, and then stir in two teaspoons of simple syrup. Mrs. Lange liked it sweet. The poor old dear's sense of taste was not what it used to be, so the reason for the two teaspoons.

"Thank you, Fancy," Mrs. Lange said, taking the cup from Jolene.

Jolene went to the dresser, to fetch madam's nightgown. She'd lay it out on the bed, and then help her dress after she finished her evening drink.

Her back was to Mrs. Lange. As she rummaged through the dresser, she heard the unmistakable sound of the woman choking. She turned to see the old woman drop her cup, slip out of her chair, falling to the floor.

Jolene ran to her, falling to her knees, taking the old woman up in her arms.

"Mrs. Lange, what's wrong?"

Mrs. Lange struggled to breathe, unable to talk. There was a gurgle, becoming louder as she fought to get another breath of air into her lungs.

She looked up into Jolene's eyes. The look of fear that was on Jolene's face was washed away by the smile on Mrs. Lange's face. She knew she was dying, and was just fine with that. She had no fear. The two smiled at each other.

They say the body is the temporary home of the soul, and that the eyes are the windows. Staring into the eyes of Mrs. Lange, Jolene watched her shuffle off her mortal coil.

Jolene placed her gently down on the floor. She wished she had the strength to pick her up and place her on her bed, except she knew she couldn't. She straightened her body, smoothed out her dress, and then crossed her arms over her chest.

Looking at the cup on the floor, the spilled liquid, Jolene knew what had happened. Someone poisoned the old woman. The potion was put in the water while she roamed the house looking for whoever had called her name. They did that purposely to distract her. Who had done this? The list was short. There was only three other people it could be.

Jolene stomped down the stairs to the kitchen. There she took a lit lantern, and stormed into Nanna's room. The woman was in bed, fast asleep, she woke up startled.

"Tell me the truth," Jolene demanded. "Did you have anything to do with it?"

"Fancy, what are you doin?" Nanna asked, sitting up in bed.

"Mrs. Lange is dead. She's been murdered with poison. Someone put it in the water for her evening drink. Tell me the truth. Did you have anything to do with this? Did he make you do it?"

"I'm sorry she's dead. She was a good woman. I had nothing to do with it, I swear."

"That only leaves two others, Billy or Massa Karl," Jolene observed out loud.

"Billy? That child wouldn't hurt anyone," Nanna said.

"I agree," Jolene said. "That only leaves one other person.

Jolene turned to leave.

"Fancy, where are ya goin'?"

"Stay in bed, Nanna. Don't come out of your room, no matter what you hear."

Nanna slid back down into her bed, pulling the covers up.

Jolene tramped through the house until she got to the library. She didn't bother to knock. She just opened the door and walked in.

Karl was sitting in his arm chair, sipping brandy. He smiled up at her when she entered.

"Fancy, I've been expecting you," he said, sounding not in the least surprised to see her barge in as she had done.

"Your grandmother is dead," Jolene announced.

"I know that. No thanks to you," he said calmly.

He took another sip of his brandy, and then reached to the table, picking up a small vile, similar to the one he gave her so many weeks ago. Holding it up, the light shone through it. Jolene saw it was half-full.

"Do you think the poison I gave you was all I purchased? I found the vile you hid in the shed, half of it is gone. If you had done what you were supposed to do, she would have been dead long ago. It only takes half a vile. I couldn't wait on you. Tonight, when I called you and you left the kitchen, I put half of my vile into the water."

Karl finished his brandy, filling the glass again.

"So, let me tell you how this is going to go down," he continued. "I am going to contact the authorities. When they get here, I will show them the body, the poisoned drink, and the half-empty vile you have hidden in your shed. They will blame you for my grandmother's death. I will morn for a few weeks. Once the will is read and all her assets are mine, I'll sell this place. I plan to travel the world. Won't that be fun?"

"I'll tell them you were the one behind it all, that you gave me the vile, forcing me to poison her. When I wouldn't do it, you took it upon yourself to do it, intending to blame me."

Karl laughed. He held up his glass in a toast to her. "Touché!" he said, and then finished off his brandy in one swallow. "I figured that's what you might do. Of course, it would be my word against a slave. Still, we don't need you spouting off, putting unnecessary doubt in their minds. So, there is more to the plan. You will not be able to tell your story to them. Do you want to know why you won't?"

Jolene nodded, waiting to hear the rest of his plan, fearing what it might be.

'You won't tell them, because you'll be dead. I'll just tell them that you tried to run away, so I was forced to shoot you."

He put down his empty brandy glass, rose from his chair, walking toward the far wall where there was a collection of guns, pistols and rifles, hung on the wall. Just as he reached out for one of the pistols, he staggered a few feet, and then fell to his knees.

"Would Massa Karl like another brandy?" a voice called from the doorway.

Jolene spun around as Karl looked up to see Billy standing there holding the vile of poison that Jolene kept hidden in the shed. It was empty.

"You're right," said Billy. "Half a vile is enough to kill. That's how much I put in your brandy."

At that moment, Karl doubled over in pain, reeling on the floor, yet, never did he stop glaring his hate at them. He began to cough, struggling to breathe.

"He's dying!" Jolene shouted. "Do something."

"It's too late," Billy said. "Let him die. Good for him. There's too much evil in the world, already. Let him die. I hope he burns in hell."

Karl was now lying on his back. Jolene fell to her knees next to him.

"You're dying," she said. "It's not too late to ask the Lord for forgiveness."

Karl laughed through the pain, and then his face went solemn.

He tried to spit in her face; only without enough air in his lungs he was unable. The spittle dripped from his mouth, down his chin. His voice was gruff, as he spoke his last words.

"For hate's sake I spit my last breath at thee."

With that, he went stiff for a moment, and then fell limp, as his last breath left his body.

"He's dead," Jolene said.

"Good," Billy replied. "We need to get out of here, fast, and get far away."

He stepped over the body to the wall. Taking down two pistols, he tucked them into his belt.

"Hurry," he said, taking Jolene by the hand, leading her out of the room and down the hall.

In the kitchen, he took a sack and began filling it with whatever food was to be found.

Nanna came walking in, carrying a lamp in front of her. She was fully dressed in her day clothes.

"What's happened?" she asked, assuming something wasn't right.

Billy answered, not looking at her as he continued to fill the sack. "Madam is dead, poisoned by Massa Karl. He's dead by the same poison. I killed him. Fancy and I are leaving. You're welcome to come with us."

Nanna placed the lamp on the table and sat down. "No, I'm too old to make a run for it. Ya two go on ahead. Besides, I had nothin' to do with it."

Billy stopped for a moment. "Ya can blame it all on me," he advised her. "But I want ya to do me a favor. If they ask about Fancy, tell 'em I forced her to go with me." He looked to Jolene. "That way, if we get caught, they'll only hang me."

"No," Jolene protested. "I'm going of my own free will. I had just as much to do with this as you did."

"Did ya?" he said. "Ya never poisoned anyone; I did. Now, take this sack, while I fill up another one."

Nanna followed them outside. Billy got the buggy ready.

"Nanna, ya can't stay here alone with two dead bodies. Ya need to take the buggy and go tell the authorities. Fancy and I will go on horseback." He looked at Jolene. "Can ya ride a horse?"

Jolene shook her head that she couldn't.

"Well, ya gonna have to learn, quickly.

He helped Nanna up onto the buggy.

"Just follow the road goin' south. Don't forget, tell 'em I did all the killin' and that I took Fancy with me at gunpoint."

Nanna looked to Jolene. "Ya take care, girl."

Jolene ran to her, the two women embraced.

"God bless ya, Nanna."

"God bless ya, too, child."

Nanna slapped the rains, driving off, never looking back.

Billy brought two horses out from the barn, and saddled them.

"Always mount on the left side of the horse," he instructed her. "Ya put ya foot here and ya hand here, and then pull ya'self up."

She did as he instructed. It took a few tries; she eventually got on.

"We'll go slowly at first till ya get the feel of it. As soon as ya do, we'll step up the pace."

When they got to the road, they both looked back. The mansion stood silently like a cold gray headstone.

"They should burn the place down," Billy declared. "Burn it down and burn the ashes."

They didn't speak till they were further up the road, going north.

"Billy, I've got a confession to make."

He didn't answer, he just listened.

"My name's not Fancy; it's Jolene…Jolene Fairchild."

Now, he looked at her.

"My name's Jolene; I'm wanted for murder."

Billy started laughing.

"Ain't we two peas in a pod?"

They began riding forward again, still moving slowly.

"Billy, where are we going?"

"To Limbo…"

"Limbo…what's that?"

"It's the place ya stay before ya get to heaven."

Chapter Twelve

One Day in Limbo

In time, Jolene could ride a horse well enough for them to move faster and farther each day.

"Seems you're gettin' the hang of it, Fancy…I mean Jolene," Billy laughed.

She smiled at him.

They got along well. At night they'd lie by the campfire, talking, getting to know each other. It was a comfortable and caring friendship. Yet it made Jolene uncomfortable, a feeling of guilt she couldn't shake off. She knew how he felt about her. She wished she could reciprocate, except it just wasn't there.

One night after they'd finished eating, both of them sat staring into the fire. The night was quiet, the stars twinkled up above. The warmth of the flame made her sleepy. From the corner of her eye, she saw something move. Without turning her head, she knew it was Billy moving in closer to kiss her.

"Don't, please," she whispered, never taking her gaze from the fire.

Again, from the corner of her eye, she saw him move away. She turned to see him lying down to sleep, his back to her.

"Sorry," she said softly, knowing it was no consolation to him.

Watching him sleep, she thought how strange relationships could be. She remembered how strongly she loved Graham. He was everything to her, though he turned on her, hurting her beyond belief. She would always recall how she felt. Here was a handsome young man, a gentle soul, who treated her with respect and caring. Yet still, she could not be swayed to love him in the manner he loved her. Was it foolishness to turn down such a love? The heart wants what the heart wants.

****

"How much farther is this place," Jolene asked as they rode along.

"I don't know," Billy said. "I've never been there. I'm only goin' by what folks have told me. I don't even know if it's true."

"That doesn't sound very promising," she said. "Exactly, what is this place suppose to be?"

"I'm really not sure," he replied.

"So, it's a place you don't know if it is; where it is, or what it is."

"When you put it that way, it *doesn't* sound very promising," he said, laughing. They both laughed, as they rode on. And why not, as far as they knew the worst was behind them?

A few hours later, Jolene felt tired. "Can we stop for a while?"

Billy was lost in thought. "If what I've been told, we should be close. Let's keep going just a little farther."

Late in the afternoon, they came to the top of a large hill. As they came over the crest, they were blinded for a moment by the golden rays of the setting sun. Looking down at the valley below, they saw a large plantation.

"That's got to be it," Billy declared. "This is where I was told it would be."

"Are you sure?" Jolene asked, clearly worried.

"There's only one way to find out," he said, starting down the slope, Jolene close behind.

When they got to the road leading onto the property, they stopped in front of an overhanging sign. There was a single word, written in large letters.

"What does it say?" Billy asked, pointing to the sign.

"It says *Limbo*," Jolene said. "We're here."

Riding down the thoroughfare, they were flanked on both sides by cotton fields.

"That's strange," Billy remarked. "These are well-groomed fields, but ain't nobody workin' them. I never heard of a plantation that didn't work their slaves till sundown, if not later."

Ahead were a main house, a barn, and a large compound with multiple long buildings. They could see people moving about. When they approached, a man halted them. He was a large black man with a big smile, obviously a fieldworker by the way he dressed.

"Welcome, brother. Welcome, sister. Welcome to Limbo."

"I don't know if where at the right place. We heard that…"

"Oh, it's the right place, all right," the man interjected. "Yes, sir, this is the right place. Ya can leave your horses near the barn. I'll have one of the boys see to 'em. Ya can come with me."

After dismounting, a barefoot boy took their horses and led them into the barn.

"I don't understand," Billy said. "How does this all work?"

"Ya need to see Brother Theodore and Sister Alice. They'll explain everything and get ya settled. Right this way."

He led them to the main house. It was not as grand as some mansions in the south, although it was still impressive.

Standing on the porch, the man introduced himself. "My name is Henry, but everyone here calls each other brother or sister. I'm one of the foremen."

"Foremen...?" Billy asked, sounding surprised.

"Yeah, we ain't got no overseers here. No whips, chains, cages. This here is God's plantation. Brother Theodore and Sister Alice just run it for Him."

"Who are Brother Theodore and Sister Alice?" Jolene asked.

"They is the right and left hand of the Lord. As I heard it, he was a white preacher from up north. He and his wife, Alice, came down south to fight against slavery. That's how they came up with the idea of Limbo, the last step before paradise, before freedom."

"But how...?" Jolene asked.

"They can explain it better than me," he concluded.

He took off his straw hat, holding it in one hand; he knocked on the front door with the other. A moment later, the door opened. A young black woman stood before them with a smile as wide as the doorway.

"Yes, brother, how may I help you?"

"We got us two new converts. They need to see the Brother and Sister."

"Of course," said the young woman. "Please, follow me."

Henry smiled good-bye, motioning for them to enter and follow her. They nodded good-bye to him, entering the home.

The inside was far grander than the outside, with finery wherever they looked. They followed the woman to a large dining room. There was a middle-aged white couple seated, one on each end of a long table.

"Sorry to bother you during your meal, but we found these two orphans left on our doorstep."

The couple stood up. They both were dressed very plain. He was slender, his hair full and white. He too had that large contagious smile.

She was a small woman, like a play doll. Her eyes were dark like buttons, and of course, a wide smile.

He rushed from his seat, across the room to them. He shook both their hands.

"Welcome…welcome." He looked to the young woman. "Sister, set up plates for our new brother and sister."

"Yes, Brother Theodore," she said, leaving the room.

The woman came to them, shaking hands with them, also.

"This is my wife, Alice, Sister Alice, and I'm Brother Theodore. Please, sit down. You must be hungry."

The next moment, Jolene and Billy were seated and eating. Their benefactors seemed more content to sit back, smiling, watching them eat. When they were nearly done, they began to question Jolene and Billy. It was all done in a friendly manner, but thorough.

"So what are your names?" Alice asked.

"My name is Billy, and this here's Jolene."

"Are you two married?"

"Oh no, ma'am, we're not."

"We're just friends," Jolene added, not wanting them to think anything of the sort.

"Well, that's good," Theodore said. "A person can't have too many friends. How is it you came to us?"

"We're runaways," Billy said, hoping that would suffice, so they wouldn't ask any more questions. He quickly changed the subject. "Please, sir, there's been so many rumors about Limbo. Please, tell us your story."

It seemed Billy had hit the right nerve. Theodore lit up like a hurricane lamp, beaming as he told their tale.

"I met Alice while I was in seminary; we fell in love, and married once I graduated. My first post was to be pastor of a small church in Georgetown, New York. It was a good life not very prosperous, but satisfying."

"We tried desperately to have children, only the Lord had other ideas for us," Alice added. Theodore wasn't put off by this rabbit trail, and trudged on.

"While we lived there, we met a most remarkable woman, a free black woman who owned a farm not far from us. I don't remember her name, but everyone called her *Minty*.

She worked with the Underground Railroad, bringing slaves to her farm where they worked for a time till they had enough money to make a go of it on their own.

"Being wholeheartedly against slavery, Alice and I were enthralled with the idea. Only we thought, instead of offering opportunity at the end of the journey, why not at the beginning? So, we came south, bought this property, and called it Limbo."

Alice took over the story from there. "Limbo is a plantation; it doesn't look unlike any other plantation, but there are major differences."

Theodore took the story from there. "All the workers are runaway slaves. They are free the moment they step on our soil, just like you two are now free. Each person lives and works here and are paid for their labors. After a year, they are paid in full, and delivered to the Underground Railroad. They go north with full pockets to start a new life."

"What if someone wants to stay longer than a year?" Billy asked.

"We'd like to offer that," Theodore said, "but new runaways arrive every month. Thank God, we are not well-know, but word does get around. We need to make room for the newcomers."

"We work six days a week, starting at sunup till five," Alice stated. "Sundays are a day of rest, starting with church service conducted by my husband," she said with pride. "We have accommodations for married couples with families. Since you are both single, Brother Billy, you will stay in the men's bunkhouse, Sister Jolene in the women's."

Just then, Henry appeared again through the kitchen door. "Are they ready, sir?"

"Brother Henry, take Brother Billy to the men's quarters and Sister Jolene to the women's." He stood up, as did Alice. Thinking it the proper thing to do, Jolene and Billy stood up, also. "Brother Henry will help you get settled. If you have any questions, he'll be glad to answer them." Again, he and Alice shook their hands in welcome. "We will see you early in the morning. Welcome to Limbo."

****

Both the men's and women's quarters were exactly the same, a long building with rows of single beds on both sides with a walkway down the center. In the center of the room was a stove for heat and making coffee. It was still early, in both bunkhouses folks were socializing as they got ready for sleep.

"Welcome, brother, what's your name?" they asked.

"The name's Billy. Tell me is this place on the up and up?"

"I know what you're thinkin'," said one of the men. "It sounds too good to be true, but it is. Every month, someone gets their year's pay, and off they go with the Underground Railroad headin' north."

"It's a miracle," said another man. "God bless Brother Theodore and Sister Alice."

It was the same in the women's quarters. Jolene was greeted by smiling faces. The women crowded around, asking questions, giving answers. All the answers were positive, comforting. Seeing that Jolene only had what was on her back; many of them gave her spare pieces of clothing. Jolene went to sleep, dizzy from all the attention. She couldn't remember a time when she felt so welcomed, so safe. Lying on her bed, she closed her eyes, praying a prayer of thanksgiving and praise before she drifted off.

****

In the morning, no one's mood changed, all was smiles and laughter. There was an area in the bunkhouses for washing. Once outside, men and women were allowed to socialize. Jolene immediately looked for Billy.

"So, how was it?" Billy asked her.

"Just fine, everyone is so nice."

"Yes, I know," he responded, sounding unsure.

Outside, long tables were set up for breakfast. Jolene and Billy sat next to each other. There was a smaller head table were Brother Theodore and Sister Alice sat. When they stood, the others followed suit. Jolene was startled for a moment when she felt a hand slip into hers. They were all joining hands.

"Dear Lord," Theodore shouted, the others went silent. "Dear Lord, thank you for this day, for this food, may we work hard for you glory. Amen!"

The crowd echoed 'Amen'. Everyone sat down, the socializing resumed. Obviously preordained, Brother Henry sat across from Jolene and Billy.

"So, what do you think?" Henry asked.

"It seems too good to be true," Billy replied. "I found that usually when something is too good to be true, it isn't."

Henry laughed. "I'm sorry ya feel that way. I hope we can change your mind. After a few months, I'm sure you won't be so untrusting."

"That makes me wonder," Billy said. "What if I don't want to stay here a year, what if I want to leave sooner?"

"No one's forcing ya to stay. Ya can leave anytime ya want," Henry said with pride.

"And your pay, what about your pay?" Billy asked.

"Ya leave without it, if ya leave before the end of a year."

"Why is that?" Jolene questioned.

"We can't have people coming and going whenever they feel like it. Paying them at the end of a year makes people commit to a year."

"How much is the pay?"

"The pay is twenty dollars a month, which y'all get in silver when ya leave."

"How long have you been here?" Jolene asked.

"Five years, but I am a foreman."

There seemed to be nothing left to talk about, for the moment. They stopped asking questions, returning to their meal.

The food was good, and plenty of it. The mood was joyous and friendly. When everyone finished, they left the tables to be cleaned by a kitchen crew. Off they walked to the fields to work. As they walked they sang hymns of praise and joyful thanksgiving. The break for lunch was similar to breakfast, good food, good company. The afternoon was more of the same, singing their way through hard work.

Looking around, Billy was surprised, he'd never seen folks work so hard, slave or free. Not these people, they worked with all their heart and soul. They worked for their freedom, for their beloved Brother Theodore and Sister Alice, for Almighty God. There wasn't anything they wouldn't do. Whatever asked of them, they did it with all their strength. They put out double fold of what Billy would believe capable of so small a group, for there was no more than a hundred folks working, not counting the twenty some odd children.

At the end of the workday, everyone returned to the compound. They washed up, getting ready for supper.

Again, they were given a hearty meal, preceded by a prayer of grace said by Brother Theodore.

After supper, folks socialized, children played, there was laughter and song till it was time to retire for the night.

Before going to the single men's quarters, Billy looked about for Jolene. He found her talking with a group of women outside the single women's bunkhouse.

"We need to talk," he whispered, pulling her off alone.

"What's wrong?" she asked.

"I think we should leave."

Jolene laughed. "Leave, for what reason?"

"I don't know. It doesn't sit well with me. Call it a feelin'."

Jolene shook her head. "I don't understand you. You dream of coming here, and when you get here, you want to leave. This has been a wonderful day. In a year's time, we'll leave free with money in our pockets. I don't understand you. Everyone here is so nice."

"That's just it, they're too nice. I've never been around folks that are this happy and friendly. It makes me uncomfortable."

"Billy, listen to me. These folks are God's people. They're filled with the Spirit. That's why they're so happy and friendly."

"I hope you're right," Billy said as he walked off to the single men's quarters.

Thirteen

Grief

Jolene woke to the chatter of women. Without opening her eyes, she knew she slept later than the days before. It was Sunday. Opening her eyes, she saw women dashing about, looking in mirrors, primping themselves.

"Get up, Sister Sleepyhead. Service is in an hour," someone laughed, the others laughed along with her. It was not said maliciously. The largest part of the jest was they all inwardly felt an hour is far too little for a woman to bring herself up to her own high standards.

Jolene sat on the edge of her bed, rubbing her eyes. She noticed a familiar aroma in the air. It made her salivate.

"What do I smell?" she asked out loud.

"Brisket," said one of the women. "Slow cooked over hot coals all nightlong with all the fixin's. But first Praise and Worship. Get along, now, sister."

Everyone assembled outside, dressed in their Sunday best. They all stood before the main house. Jolene looked to find Billy. They stood next to each other.

"Are ya all right?" he whispered.

Jolene seemed put-off by his constant mistrust of the situation. "We worked the entire week. True, I can't remember when I worked harder. But I'm eating better than ever, sleeping better than ever. These people are good people. I've never been treated this good in all my life. Whatever it is that's bothering you, you need to let it go."

"Perhaps, ya right."

"You need to be thankful. Thank God for what you've got."

Just then, everyone broke out in song. They sang with all their might, with deep feeling. In the middle of the fourth hymn, Brother Theodore and Sister Alice stepped out onto the porch. Both dressed in what most folks would call Church clothes. They held their Bibles to their chests, over their hearts.

When the hymn ended, everyone went silent. Brother Theodore stepped forward to the edge of the porch. The bright sun shining in his eyes caused him to squint.

"Brothers and sisters, I ask you what is love. We talk about it, dream about it, sing about it, hunger for it, live and die for it. You can't see it, smell it, taste it, or hold it in your hands. We all believe in it, but I doubt if one person here could tell me what it is. That's because there are no words to describe it.

"It's the same thing with God. We talk about Him, worship Him, read about Him, and sing about Him. Just like love, you don't see Him, or hear Him. You believe in Him. Still, no one can fully know Him. The Good Book says God is Love. Well, don't that beat all? We're lost for words about both of them, then we find out it's not two things, but one. That's why both are a mystery.

"We need to put God first in our lives, make Him part of our lives. I'm not talking religion. I'm talking about a one-on-one relationship. If not, all is lost, we will never progress. We try to think that we do, but that's a falsehood man has always believed. That he could do it on his own.

"Since the beginning, man has sacrificed, fasted, and prayed, yet he remains the same. If you were to go back in time, sit around a fire with cavemen, looking into their eyes, I bet you'd recognize every one of them. Because none of these things can change you, only God can."

Led by the Spirit, Brother Theodore preached for another ten minutes. However, he was no fool. He knew folks can only stand and listen for so long. He saw the children were getting antsy. He too could smell the barbecue.

"Let me finish by asking the Lords blessing on all here today. Blessing on all here and on the bounty we are about to receive. Amen!"

"Amen," they all echoed.

What came next could only be described as a church picnic. More good food than they could eat in three days. Children ran and played. The atmosphere was festive with talking and laughing, and later music with singing and dancing.

Jolene was pleased to see Billy smiling, enjoying himself. He was finally letting down his guard, allowing the magic of the place and time to wash over him. She was also pleased to see how many young women made a fuss over him, some out-and-out flirting with him. Perhaps, in time, his crush on her would be forgotten.

****

Once a month, after Sunday service, instead of the usual church picnic, everyone was taken in wagons to the banks of the Des Mensonges River, a short five miles from Limbo.

Other than the location, it was the same church picnic they held ever Sunday, except instead of benches, folks lay on blankets spread out on the riverbank.

Late in the afternoon, when the heat of the day was its strongest, everyone stood on the banks to witness the monthly baptisms. Brother Theodore, dressed in a flowing white robe, waded out to waist-high water. One by one, those to be baptized, also dressed in white robes, waded out to Brother Theodore.

Jolene stood in the back of the crowd. Unable to see, she worked her way to the front of the gathering. To her surprise, she saw Billy making his way in the water to Brother Theodore.

"Do you believe in God, the forgiveness of sin, and the resurrection?" Brother Theodore shouted for all to hear.

"Yes, I do," Billy announced.

"Then I baptize you in the name of the Father, Son, and Holy Ghost."

With that, Billy held his nose, as Brother Theodore dunked him under. When he came up, he jumped for joy; the crowd cheered, and then broke into song.

Jolene was so happy for him. She was also relieved to see Billy sharing a blanket with a very pretty young woman. She let out a sigh of relief. Finally, they could be friends.

****

Three months into her stay at Limbo, life became routine. The days were good, flowing into each other in a natural order. Life was good, which is why what occurred one morning, confused Jolene and many others.

Jolene woke with a jolt. Opening her eyes, it was still dark, just before sunrise. Becoming more aware, she realized what woke her. Outside, on the compound, echoed the sound of a woman screaming. It was a constant scream, full of fear.

Others woke. It became mayhem as women scrambled around her, rushing to and fro, getting dressed. Jolene got out of bed, and quickly put on her clothes. They all rushed out, as did the single men and those from the family building.

The lights were lit in the main house. A moment later, Theodore and Alice rushed out of the house, running to the others at the center of the compound.

There was a woman in her nightgown, screaming in terror at the top of her lungs. She was pointing at the barn.

Following her gaze, seeing what she saw, many of the other women began to scream, as well. On the second story of the barn, dangling from a rope tied to the loading post was the limp dead body of a young woman. It was clear, she'd hanged herself. Why would anyone commit suicide in Limbo?

Moving in for a closer look, Jolene recognized the woman. It was Missy, the young housekeeper at the main house, the woman they met the day they came to Limbo, who'd served them their meal. Jolene didn't know her well, although she saw her nearly everyday. She seemed to be happy all the time, content with her work and her life. What had brought her to this point?

Some of the men went into the barn, from the opening on the second level they reached out, taking hold of the rope. They reeled her in, and then taking the noose from off her neck. A moment later, they brought her down, placing the body on the ground in front of the barn.

Brother Theodore called from the porch, "Brothers and sisters, gather round."

Feeling uncomfortable in the moment, no longer wishing to look at the body, the people gathered in front of the porch.

"Brothers and sisters, this is a sad day," Brother Theodore said. "There is only one thing you can do with such grief, and that is to turn your back on it and walk away. I want everyone to go back to your homes, get ready for the day, and start working in the fields. We'll discuss this later."

Silently with heads bowed, they retuned to dress for the day. There was no breakfast that morning, not that anyone felt like eating. They sang as they walked to the fields. Hymns of sadness were sung for the rest of the day.

Lunchtime came and went, none was served. No one so much as mentioned it. They continued laboring. Working, keeping busy, allowed them to move forward without dwelling on their loss, on their sorrow.

When they returned from their workday, the benches and tables were set, ready for supper. Of course, the body of the young woman was gone, though they looked at the spot in front of the barn like it was a holy shrine.

Brother Henry stood on the porch of the main house.

"Brothers and sisters," he shouted. Everyone stopped and waited. "Today has been a sorrowful day. Brother Theodore and Sister Alice will not be with us tonight. They have vowed to fast and pray through the night. We need to put this behind us. Everyone, go and get ready for supper."

One of the women called out, "Where is Missy? What happened to the body?"

"She's already been buried," Brother Henry announced.

"Why? We wanted to be a part of her burial," someone said.

"Brother Theodore thought it best not to dwell on our loss. We need to move on. He thought it best for all."

"Where did they bury her, so we can pay our respects?" asked another.

"She was buried in a secret grave that is not on the property," Brother Henry answered.

"Why?" asked a few.

"Suicide is a sin. It is a grievous offense against the Lord. Missy died in her sin. She could not be buried in hollow ground."

They stood silent with painful looks on their faces.

Henry stepped forward. "Forget this, move on, y'all get ready for supper."

Fourteen

One Year in Limbo

The next day, after breakfast, as everyone was on their way to the fields to work, Henry stopped Jolene.

"I've been asked to take ya to the house. Brother Theodore and Sister Alice want to speak with ya."

"About what...?" Jolene asked.

Henry shrugged his shoulders. "Ya got me. That's for them to know and tell ya, not me."

In the main house, Henry walked Jolene to the back parlor. Brother Theodore was there, alone.

"I brought ya Sister Jolene, like ya asked."

"Very good, brother," Theodore said, rushing to them. "You can go now."

Henry nodded, turned and left. When they heard the front door close, Theodore approached her.

"Sister Jolene, have you been happy here with us?"

"Oh, yes, sir, very much so."

"Good, good," he said, stepping over to the window. "Come here, Jolene, step into the light let me get a better look at you."

She walked across the room toward him. The sunlight poured over her. He eyed her carefully.

"You're a very beautiful young woman, Jolene."

"Thank you, sir."

"The reason why I called you here is because I have a splendid idea that will benefit us both."

Jolene remained silent, listening.

"It's a tragic shame what happened yesterday with Missy. She will be missed. In the meantime, we have no one working the kitchen. I've been told you have experience. Would you like the job? It is easier than working in the fields."

"Sir, I don't know what to say. Yes, I would like to. It would be an honor."

"Good, good, you can start in the morning. My wife will go over everything, so you know the way we like things." He took hold of both of her hands, smiling into her eyes. "You've made me so very happy today, my dear."

Jolene was filled with joy. Over the last few months, he had become a father figure to her, someone she respected and wanted to aspire to be like.

They remained standing, facing each other, holding hands for an overly long time, long enough that Jolene began feeling uncomfortable.

"Yes, very happy, my dear," he repeated, pulling her in close to him.

Jolene was afraid he was going to kiss her, he didn't. He just brought her in, putting his arms around her tightly, hugging her.

"You're such a sweet child," he whispered in her ear.

The moment felt awkward; she didn't know what to do. She was afraid of offending him. After all, he really wasn't doing anything wrong. Perhaps, he was simply a highly emotional soul.

They remained in this position, when suddenly the door opened. In walked his wife, Alice. He let Jolene loose, backing away from her like a spider jumps off a hot grill.

"Alice, darling, you came at just the right moment. Sister Jolene, here, has consented to be our cook."

"How nice," Alice proclaimed.

Jolene felt ashamed. His wife had walked in on them while in an embrace. She didn't seem the least put off about it. Clearly, it was all very innocent. How could she have doubted this sweet old man?

"Theodore, my love, we need to let this poor girl go. She has a full day of work ahead of her." She looked to Jolene. "I'll see you in the morning."

"Yes, ma'am, thank you."

Jolene left the main house, walking to the fields, feeling blissfully happy.

****

Unfortunately, Jolene's first suspicions were on the mark. Brother Theodore was not the father figure she'd hoped for. She called him brother, he called her sister; however that didn't seem the way he viewed their relationship.

When the opportunity rose, he would take it. If they passed one another in the hall, in that brief moment his hands were all about her. She never knew when he would come into the kitchen under the false pretense of wanting to know what was for dinner; again, he'd molest her. His hands would wander over her in places only a husband, sanctioned by holy matrimony, would dare venture.

She didn't know what to do. If she screamed, she could only imagine the chaos that would ensue. Who could she tell? Who could she go to? Life at Limbo was good. Everyone was so content. She could only see in her mind's eye what such accusations would do to the lives of the people around her, people she'd grown to love. Besides, it would be his word against her. She doubted if she would prevail. She could leave, runaway, except where would she go, and how. No, the only solution she could think of was to let the old man have his way. Her only hope was that he would not take matters any further than fondling. She prayed every night for an answer. Strangely enough, the answer came from Brother Theodore.

Once a week, Sister Alice would inspect the children's facility where the children too young to work were kept by some of the elderly women who were too old to work the fields. The too young and the too old spend their days together. It was Sister Alice's pet project to see that all was well. On the days of her visits this was when Jolene dreaded the most. Being alone in the house with Brother Theodore was a scenario for disaster. It was on such a day, Brother Theodore asked her to join him in the parlor. Jolene did so, reluctantly.

"Jolene, we need to talk. I am the spiritual leader here at Limbo. Nevertheless, I'm still a man. I still sin like the rest of the world. I don't want to; only my sinful nature is strong. Prayer and fasting are my only weapons."

He fell to his knees at her feet, crying as he spoke. "Dear child, you must help me. Please, pray for my soul. When the devil takes hold of me, I can't help myself. I only see your beauty. It is like I am possessed. Oh, Jolene, please forgive me, pray for me. If I ever touch you, again, pray all the harder that the moment will pass. Together we can defeat this demon. Oh, dear sister, have mercy on me, pray for me."

"Of course I will, brother," she said from her heart.

"Thank you and bless you," he said, taking her apron and kissing its hem.

She left him on his knees, returning to the kitchen, smiling. Her faith in Brother Theodor, the entire world, was restored.

****

Every night as she lay in bed, Jolene prayed for Brother Theodore's redemption. It is not an easy task to overcome temptation. She knew this, which is why she endured in silence his moments of weakness, his backsliding.

On days when they were the only two in the house, he would come into the kitchen, sneak up behind her, and take hold of her.

"Brother, please, do not forget yourself!" Jolene warned.

"Pray for me, child, pray louder!" he'd scream into her ear.

It was no use. The louder she prayed, the more excited he'd get. He would rub up against her like a dog until his body went stiff and he would collapse to the floor in ecstasy. Jolene would help him up, guiding him to the parlor. She'd drop him onto the settee, where he would pass out, sleeping it off like a drunk.

The one shining light in all of this was that through Jolene's constant prayer and fasting, these episodes happened less with each week. In time, it was only a monthly occurrence. Yet, sadly, it continued for months.

****

It was the anniversary of Jolene's and Billy's arrival to Limbo. A full year passed. It was a year of hope. Excluding, the incident with Missy, and a few mishaps Jolene had with Brother Theodore, which she told no one about. They had seen many people come and go in that time. Now, it was their turn to leave.

On a Sunday, after morning service, during the usual church picnic, Brother Theodore shouted from the main house porch. His bride, Sister Alice, was by his side.

"May I have your attention, please? Today we lift up our Brother Billy. He has been with us a year, now. He is a good worker and a good man. Although, we will miss him, it is time for him to leave. Billy, could you please come up here?"

Billy stepped onto the porch, standing between Theodore and Alice. Brother Theodore held up a small pouch for everyone to see.

"A year's wages in silver to get you started in your new life," he announced as he handed Billy the pouch. "Brother Henry will guide you to the Underground Railroad within the hour."

Everyone cheered, as Billy and Theodore shook hands. Alice hugged and kissed him. Billy held up the pouch of silver to more cheers.

Brother Henry stood next to Jolene. He bent low, speaking into her ear, over the shouts of the others.

"I can only take one person at a time to the Underground Railroad. Don't worry; you will be the next to go."

"When…?" Jolene asked.

"Soon…don't worry."

Jolene felt disappointed, still she smiled, happy for Billy. Inwardly, she wondered why she was not chosen to go before Billy. Perhaps, Brother Theodore had a hand in all of it. In his weakness, doing what he could to keep her near. No, that couldn't be. She shook off the disgusting thought.

Later, when everyone was enjoying their meal, Billy came to Jolene.

"I have to go, now," he said, smiling into her eyes. "I will never forget ya, never."

"I will pray for you everyday," she said, smiling back.

They reached out to each other. They hugged. Jolene kissed his cheek. Stepping back, he touched the spot she had kissed, as if it were a precious gift.

Amidst the noise and laughter, Jolene stood silently, nearly in tears, as she watched Billy and Brother Henry walk down the road, away from Limbo till they were out of sight.

Fifteen

Leaving Limbo

It had been a month since Billy left Limbo. Her time to leave would be soon. Nothing was said to her about it. She never complained. It was all in God's hands. Besides, life was good. She enjoyed her work. Everyone around her was friendly and positive. Best of all, the outbursts of Brother Theodore's passions, the incidents occurred seldom. She had hopes that if she prayed hard enough, long enough, they would disappear all together.

It was a well-known fact, Theodore and Alice had a business partner, Theodore's younger brother, Vincent.

Vincent was nearly twenty-years Theodore's junior. A younger, handsome version of his older brother, with dark good looks, slender built, and always well-dressed.

He lived in New Orleans. All harvested cotton from Limbo was sent to his warehouse. From there he would do all the wheeling and dealing, selling the bales of cotton to the highest bidders. He sold cotton to all parts of the country as well as out of the country, through the harbors of New Orleans. He was good at his job.

Each year, he would visit his brother and sister-in-law. His trips to Limbo had a dual-purpose, to discuss business, and simply a family visit.

This year, there was a third reason to come to Limbo. Thirty-five year old Vincent, a long-established bachelor, finally decided to tie the knot. He'd come to show off his new bride, Effie.

Effie Sauvageon was well-known throughout the city of New Orleans, only for all the wrong reasons. She was mostly known by the police for her many antics, both misdemeanor and felony, from petty theft to murder and everything in between. Though through bribery, both financial and the use of her many womanly charms, she was never convicted. She never so much as saw a prison cell.

Still, Effie held one dream in her life. That was to be rich and accepted by the upper crust of New Orleans' society. Her marriage to Vincent made her dream flesh. She could now afford her heart's desire, dine at the finest restaurants, and be invited to all the women's clubs, galas and social events her lowly class was excluded from.

She didn't love Vincent. She found him tolerable. To be honest, Vincent didn't love her either. Her beauty, the body of a goddess, an angelic face framed by the brightest of blonde hair, made her the jewel of all his possessions. For all practical purposes, Effie and Vincent were well suited for each other.

The day the newlyweds arrived, they were shown to their room at the main house where they could freshen up. After which, they were given the grand tour of Limbo with Theodore and Alice.

Jolene was in the kitchen that day earlier than other days. There was much to do for the dinner Alice planned for their guests, in celebration of their recent nuptials. The finest meats available in the county were purchased. Vegetables were slowly cooked, pastries baked and cooled. Contributing to the festivities, Vincent brought a case of fine French wine with him from New Orleans. Jolene never knew Brother Theodore and Sister Alice drank wine. She assumed it was against their religious beliefs. Then again, wine is mentioned in the Bible, and besides, this was a special occasion.

It was midafternoon when they returned from the tour. The foursome opened the first of many bottles of the wine Vincent brought. It wasn't long before their loud laughter filled the entire house.

Sister Alice stormed into the kitchen with her new best friend and sister-in-law, Effie. The two women were laughing hysterically.

"How much longer till supper?" Alice asked.

"Oh, ma'am, it won't be for another hour," Jolene answered.

The two women continued laughing, as if everything was a joke.

"An hour…!" Effie exclaimed. "But, I'm hungry, now."

Alice took a loaf of bread sitting on the table, pulled off a piece, handing it to Effie. "Here, have some bread."

Effie took the piece, hurling it across the room. "I don't want bread. I want cake. Let them eat cake!"

They both thought this hilarious, screaming with laughter as they left the kitchen.

An hour later, Jolene set the table, placing the food out, as well. The foursome entered the dining room.

"Why, Sister Jolene, you've outdone yourself," Theodore said, "You've worked so hard all-day. Why don't you put the deserts out on the sideboard, we'll serve ourselves, you can take the rest of the day off."

Jolene went into the kitchen; put the deserts on a tray, returning to the dining room. They were all seated.

"Is there anything else, Brother Theodore?" Jolene asked after she placed the tray on the sideboard.

"No, Sister Jolene, thank you very much. You may leave, now."

Jolene curtsied, turned and left.

"Pretty little thing," Vincent commented.

Effie jokingly kicked him from under the table.

"Ouch...that wasn't necessary," he laughed.

In their drunkenness, they were so loud; Jolene was able to hear them all the way to the single women's quarters. Many of the women were quietly lounging about, getting ready for sleep.

Jolene sat on the edge of her bed. It felt good to get off her feet. She was just about to lie down when a thought came to her. She wasn't sure; she might have left the kettle on the stove. In time, the water would steam away, the kettle would be ruined. She got up from her bed, heading back to the main house.

In the kitchen, she realized she was right. She had left the kettle on. Taking a towel, she took the kettle off the stove. There was no laughter coming from the dining room, just soft whispers. Jolene went to the kitchen door. She was just about to enter the dining room to see if they needed anything when she heard Vincent.

"This place is a gold mine," Vincent announced.

"I don't understand," Effie said. "What's the difference between this plantation and others?"

"It's simple," Brother Theodore said. "All plantations use slave labor, we don't. We promise these runaway slaves a year's wage and a ride on the Underground Railroad to freedom."

"I still don't understand," Effie insisted.

Theodore continued, "You can enslave someone, force them to labor, but no matter what you do to them they will never work as hard as you'd want them to. Our people here at Limbo work like there's no tomorrow. They work themselves to near death. Our output is triple that of other plantations."

"There's one thing wrong with your plan," Effie claimed. "Paying them a year's wage and seeing they get north has got to eat into your profit."

Alice laughed, "That's the angle. No one get's anything except an early grave. We pay them in front of everyone to keep up appearances. Once we have them off the property, we kill them and take back the money."

"Why do you kill them?" Effie asked. "Why not sell them and double your money."

"And have them talk?" Theodore added. "We need slaves to believe Limbo is what they've heard it is. Runaways come to us constantly. That's the reason we only allow for them to stay a year; we need to make room for the newcomers."

"That's genius," Effie laughed, "sheer genius."

"Oh, my God," Jolene whispered in shock, backing away from the door, hitting the table behind her. An empty bottle of wine fell off the table, rolling across the floor.

"What was that?" Theodore exclaimed, running to the kitchen. He entered just in time to see from the window Jolene running off across one of the fields.

He rushed back to the dining room.

"What's wrong?" Vincent asked.

Theodore didn't answer. He hurried to his office, returning a moment later with two pistols.

"That blasted girl, the cook, she heard everything. She's making a run for it. We've got to stop her."

He handed one of the guns to his brother.

"Vincent, you come with me." He looked to his wife. "Alice, go tell Henry and his men what happened. I saw her running north."

"What should I do?" Effie asked.

"Go with Alice," Vincent commanded. "Keep a light burning in the window. We won't be long."

****

Darkness was all around. Being a moonless night, moving about was difficult. Jolene stumbled and fell many times. The only benefit the darkness offered was that when she looked back she could see the fiery torches of her pursuers.

If she stayed to the roads, she would easily be caught. So, she ventured into the forest, which made going more difficult. Every time she looked back, she could see they were gaining on her. It all seemed so hopeless.

She heard their voices coming closer till she could make out what they were saying word for word.

"She can't be too far ahead," Theodore said.

"It doesn't matter," she heard Henry say. "The direction she's goin', she won't be able to go much farther."

What did he mean by that, 'she won't be able to go much farther'? What was up ahead that would prevent her from continuing?

A quarter mile ahead, she understood what Henry was talking about. The ground under her feet gave way becoming soft and moist. The farther on she tread, the more water oozed from the ground under her feet.

She stopped when she realized what was ahead. She was on the banks of a swamp. Murky water as far as she could see, within it trees, fallen trees, and everything covered in deep green moss.

Jolene fell to her knees, looking up to the sky. The stars sprawled across the firmament like diamonds on a black silk scarf. All that came to her mind was Psalm Fifty-nine. *Deliver me from mine enemies, O my God; defend me from them that rise up against me.*

This prayer echoed in her mind till it was overtaken by the sound of voices behind her. Looking out at the swamp before her, she had few alternatives. She could give herself up, at which time she would immediately be killed. Or she could move forward where her chances of survival were slim to none, yet still better than a bullet to the head. She had no choice. She decided to trudge onward into the swamp.

Once she stepped forward into the water she sank up to her hips. It was impossible to move quickly. Each step, her foot sunk deep into the silt and mud. It took all her strength to pull her foot up and take another step forward. When she was only a few feet in, she hid behind a tree trunk, looking back, her pursuers reached the edge of the swamp.

"We've lost her," Vincent said.

Theodore laughed, "No, this is better than I could hope for. There's only two ways out of this swamp. She can come back to us, or continue forward. No one could survive getting to the other side of this swamp. Either way, our problem is solved. Come, Vincent, let's return to the ladies and finish our evening. Henry, you stay here with your men; make sure she doesn't backtrack. I'll see you in the morning. Are you ready, Vincent?"

****

Jolene waited to catch her breath. She watched as Brother Theodore and Vincent left, leaving Brother Henry and two other men at the banks of the swamp. It was a good thing it was so dark. She was only a few feet away, so close they could have stepped in, reached out, and grabbed her.

Knowing she had to trudge on, she took a step forward. She tripped over something on the ground below. She fell forward into the water. When she came back up, she struggled to get her footing. What it was that she tripped over was not a stone. She looked into the water, watching whatever it was float to the top. As it rose to the surface, she could see it was the face of someone. The face came forward; it was the face of a black man. When the face appeared on the surface of the water, she had to bite her lip not to scream. It was Billy, long dead, buried in the swamp by Henry and his men. The face was bloated from being in the water for so long. Parts of his face were eaten away by the creatures of the swamp.

Bending down, she reached out, pulling up the body parts of others, mostly bones from skeletons of runaway slaves whose journey led them to a dead end, a cold, filthy swamp as their grave.

All those poor people who hoped, and worked themselves to near death for a promise that was never kept – a lie. This was their payment. This was their cemetery. Jolene cried as she waded on. It was so hard to believe there were such people in the world that would do this to other people. She was beginning to see the world differently. Still, she refused to change her moral ways. If anything, it made them stronger. She vowed never to stray from the Ten Commandments and righteousness.

****

It was morning, the sun filtered through the treetops. Jolene moved through the swamp the entire night with still no end in sight. She was grateful, despite a few minor cuts and bruises, she was unharmed.

Finally, midmorning she saw it, a few yards away, it was the end of the swamp. Beyond the swamp was a sunlit glen of deep green grass and marigolds. She pushed forward all the harder. Her hand was underwater, when suddenly, a sharp pain burst in her hand, traveling up her arm to her shoulder. Raising her hand out of the water, a snake was attached to her, its fangs deep in the flesh between her thumb and forefinger. She screamed in horror, waving her arm frantically till the snake lost its hold and went flying a few feet away.

She rushed with all her might toward the shore of the swamp. All her clothes were soaked, heavy with water. She struggled to stand on dry land. Her heart raced so fast and loud it was like someone beating a drum in her ears. After only a few steps into the sunlight, the world began to spin. The snake's poison hit her heart. She fell to the ground.

"Oh, Lord, if I am to die, take me, a sinner, into your sweet embrace. I long to hear you say '*Welcome, good and faithful servant*,'" she called out to the sky and sun above.

"Don't ya worry, ya ain't gonna die," said a voice.

The last thing she remembered before falling into unconsciousness was a soft, cool hand, gently caressing her forehead.

Sixteen

A Prayer in the World

Jolene woke to find herself lying on a cot in what looked like a prison cell. Her hand and arm were swollen and hurting. The metal door with a barred breach at the top opened. In walked a middle-aged black woman carrying a food tray.

"You're awake, good," the woman said, placing the tray on a small table next to the cot. "I brought ya some soup. Try to sit up. Ya haven't had anything to eat since ya got here two days ago."

"What happened?" Jolene inquired in a daze.

"My name's Gabrielle. I work here."

"Where is here?" Jolene asked.

"This is Masion de fous, it's like a hospital."

"A hospital with prison cells...?" Jolene questioned.

"Some of the patients are...how should I put this...it's a hospital for those sick in the mind, not the body. You will learn more, in time." Gabrielle sat on the edge of the bed, taking up a bowl from the tray. She offered a spoonful to Jolene. "Here, it's just clear broth, but it will do ya good."

Jolene leaned forward, taking in the warm liquid, as Gabrielle continued explaining. "My husband, Philippe, takes the cart into New Orleans once each month for supplies. He found ya on the side of the road. From the marks on your hand, he knew it was snakebite. He cut the wound and sucked the poison out. Then he brought ya here. That was two days ago."

"Am I a prisoner?" Jolene asked, pointing to the metal door.

"Oh, no," Gabrielle laughed. "We just didn't have any other place to put ya. In a day or two, ya should be feelin' better; I'll take ya to the Master."

"The Master...?" Jolene questioned, sounding apprehensive.

"Yes, Doctor La Tueur. He owns and runs the asylum.

The word asylum was not one Jolene heard often, still she knew what it meant. It gave her pause, filling her with caution.

Two days later, Jolene was feeling better. The swelling in her hand and arm had gone down, the pain was subsiding. The door to her cell opened, again. This time a tall black man entered. His arms were muscular, as was his chest. His close-cropped dark hair was going white at the temples. He smiled at Jolene as he entered.

"My name is Philippe. I've come to take ya to Doctor La Tueur's office."

"Philippe," Jolene said with surprise. "You saved my life. I can't thank you enough."

"It twasn't nothin'," he replied, humbly.

"It was to me," Jolene insisted. "God bless you, for what you did."

"Can ya walk?"

"Yes, not very fast, but I know I can."

Being bedridden for so many days, Jolene walked slowly, a little weak in the knees. Philippe kept close to her, in case she fell. They walked along the corridor of patients' rooms. All of them were exactly the same as the room she stayed in, more like prison cells. In fact, it all resembled a prison rather than a hospital.

They walked down a flight of stairs. Everything was different. There was room after room of what could only be described as a mansion with a sitting room, a library, a dining room, and a parlor. They came to a large wooden door at the end of a long hallway. Philippe knocked.

"Come in," a voice called from within.

Philippe opened the door, Jolene followed him in.

"Sir, this is the girl," Philippe said, standing at attention like a soldier.

"Thank you, Philippe, you may leave now," Doctor La Tueur said, sitting behind a large desk.

Without another word, Philippe turned and left.

"Please, take a seat," the doctor said, motioning to an armchair in front of his desk. "Are you feeling better, Jolene? That is your name, isn't it?" he asked.

"Yes, sir, thank you," Jolene answered shyly.

Doctor La Tueur was a handsome man, long and lean. Clean shaven, with black hair nearly to his shoulders. His piercing eyes were milky blue, his nose pointed sharply. He wore the finest of custom-made suits and shirts made of silk. His accent clearly proclaimed him a Frenchman. Not the musical accent, the broken Cajun twang that one so often hears in New Orleans and around Louisiana, a true French inflection.

"Tell me truthfully, child. How did you find your way to our doorstep? I warn you, if you lie, you will be found out in time, and I will turn you over to the authorities."

Jolene hesitated for a moment, and then decided to take a step forward, to tell the truth, or at least as much of it she felt comfortable giving. "I'm a runaway slave from a nearby plantation."

"I thought as much," he said. "You may have sanctuary here, for a price."

"And what is that?"

"Your loyalty and hard work is the cost. Gabrielle could use a hand in the kitchen, there's much to be done. As well, the patients need looking after. Meals must be served, bedsheets changed, chamber pots emptied, and a score of other unpleasant chores. You will have a small room just off the kitchen. That is if you accept my terms."

Jolene nodded, agreeing.

"Good," he said, smiling. "Philippe!" he called out. A moment later, Philippe entered.

"Yes, sir…"

"Jolene will be with us from now on. Take her to her room. Have your wife put her work starting tomorrow."

"Yes, sir…"

Jolene was unsure of what she had agreed to, however she had no other choice.

****

Andre La Tueur was a mystery. Little was known about him, except for a few basic facts. He was forty years old, came from France five years ago. He was a doctor. That was the extent of what the people of New Orleans knew of him. Nevertheless, to many he was considered a savoir.

La Tueur erected a hospital one hundred miles north of New Orleans. This hospital, Masion de fous, made of granite with high walls was more likened to a fort or a prison. It was what was needed at the time, in great demand.

As it was since the beginning of time, New Orleans broke into two classes, the haves and the have-nots. Poor people with mental illness did not live long, they were either locked away, mistreated, or they roamed the streets, homeless and hungry. It was different for the wealthy. Rich families would keep their ill relatives locked away in their homes, never to be seen, avoiding the embarrassment. They would see to their care, food and cleanliness. Though, without medical attention, they died off, as well, often to suicide.

La Tueur offered these wealthy families another alternative. An upscale hospital, a few days ride from the city, guaranteed care and protection of their loved one. It was expensive, but worth it. There would be no more worry or embarrassment. La Tueur even offered the possibility, through his medical program; the relative might someday be cured. This removed feelings of shame and guilt.

The La Tueur program was simple. There were never more than fifteen patients at one time. Each patient was locked in their own room, away from others. They were treated well. The guards would rotate visits to the garden where they could get exercise, sun and fresh air, though only one at a time. La Tueur believed lunacy breeds lunacy, so they were kept separate at all times.

The key to his method was twofold. Lunacy was to be seen as any other disease, no different from a cold or flu. The effects of mental illness were caused by dark humors in the blood. So, every few days, each patient would be bled a bowlful, followed by days of high quality, nutritious foods. The belief was in time the bad blood would be exchanged for good blood, in time leading to a cured, stable, clear-thinking, healthy patient. "The blood is the life," La Tueur often said. "My method is the path to sanity."

****

It was a different life for Jolene, an easy life, all in all. Her bedroom was small and neat, not any bigger than the cells they kept the patients in, though there was no metal door or lock. Most of her days she spent with Gabrielle in the kitchen. They would start the day early, cooking breakfast. They cooked the same meal for everyone, the doctor, the guards, the help, and the patients. Believing good nutrition was the key to good health, that and bloodletting, all the food was of the highest quality, prepared with great care. Lunch and supper were no different.

Between kitchen chores, Gabrielle would clean the downstairs, dusting the parlor, the library, and the office. As well, she did all the doctor's laundry, clothing and bedsheets. It made for a full day.

Jolene, on the other hand, spent her time seeing to the needs of the patients. There was laundry, clothing and bedsheets. Chamber pots needed empting and cleaning. Water jugs needed refilling. Jolene delivered all the patients' meals, collecting the dirty dishes, bringing them back to the kitchen to clean. No one was allowed knives or forks, only spoons of wood.

Jolene got along well with Gabrielle, also her husband, Philippe, though she only spent time with him at meals, which all three took together. Though she often saw Doctor La Tueur, walking from his office to the library, spending hours reading, then hours back in his office, he rarely said two words to her. Now and then he would enter the kitchen asking for a pot of tea. Jolene would prepare it and deliver it to his office. For this she received a "Thank you". Hours later she fetched the tray, again to another "Thank you", unless his face was buried in a book, when he wouldn't so much as notice her or the disappearance of the teapot.

Jolene's association with the guards was seldom and short whenever there was contact. They were a strange crew. Keeping to themselves, speaking seldom even to one another. They were very solemn men with cold stares, like a gaze, unblinking, somewhat inhuman. The only thing Gabrielle would say about these men was that they didn't need to be served their meals. They would pick up their plates from the kitchen, and return them when finished. Besides that, she neither liked nor trusted them.

As for the inmates, the patients, Jolene's contact with them was often, though always brief. She would deliver their meals through an opening at the bottom of the metal doors, a metal slit that slid open and close.

There were only twelve patients in resident, four women, eight men. Most of them were in a sad state, staring at the wall for hours, never moving or speaking. When they were brought outside into the garden, they acted no different, sitting on a bench, staring at the outer walls.

There were rare moments when the patients spoke to her. Slipping their meal under the door, sometimes the sound of the metal would catch their attention. Some would simply say "Thank you", and nothing more. Although, there were infrequent times they would try to hold a conversation with her. Kindhearted Jolene listened. Only, most of what they said was nonsensical, running the gambit from friendly to angry and everything in between. Jolene would smile and move on.

However, there was one patient who seemed different from the others. She was coherent in her speech and mannerisms, a dark haired beauty with skin as white as porcelain.

One night, Jolene looked into the small window of the women's cell. She saw no one; the woman must have been hiding in the corner. Jolene knelt down, slid back the metal, and pushed the food tray forward. Without warning, the woman grabbed Jolene by her wrist. She wanted to scream, call for one of the guards, except her fear was too great. She couldn't move or make a sound.

"You must help me," the woman whispered, letting go of Jolene. "Please, talk to me."

Right off, there were two things Jolene realized. From her tone and demeanor, the woman seemed to be rational. Also, her accent was clear, thick, and easy to spot. She was French, a woman of wealth.

"How can I help you?" Jolene asked, keeping her voice down, afraid the guards might hear.

"I must escape, you must help me. If I stay much longer, I will be killed."

Now, such talk made Jolene suspicious that she might be talking to just another delusional patient.

"Who is going to kill you?"

"My name is Georgette...Georgette La Tueur."

"La Tueur, but that's the doctor's name, the head of Masion de fous."

"That is true. He is my husband."

"No one ever said Doctor La Tueur had a wife," Jolene questioned.

"That's because no one here knows of me. Just after Andre and I married, he left to come to America to seek his fortune. It was my money that built this place. After not hearing from him for so long, I decided to come and find him. When I found him, I learned he never really loved me, it was all for the money. He locked me up with all these poor people. He wants me dead. He bleeds them every four days. He bleeds me every other day. In a few days, I will be dead. It will look like an accident, but it will be murder."

"I will pray for you," Jolene said.

"I don't need prayer. If I don't get out soon, I won't have a prayer in the world."

Seventeen

A Brief History and Observation

The early Egyptians were known for it, the Greeks at the time were keen on it, too. Bloodletting, that is. It was believed to be the cure for every disease known to man, especially headaches and fevers.

It was believed the disease remained trapped within the body. So, it made sense there needed to be a release of this humor within the body. The logical step would be bloodletting.

By the 1800s, new ideas came into play; the practice of bloodletting had fallen out of vogue with most doctors. When I say most, I mean there were a few stragglers who refused to step into the modern age. Doctor Andre La Tueur was one of the latter.

The procedure was straightforward, gory, yet simple. One by one, the guards would take one of the patients to a small room at the end of the corridor. A plain room with a small table to one side, in the center of the room was a large chair that stood high and tilted back slightly. There were straps all about to keep the patient in place, their legs, torso, head, and arms. The arms were the most peculiar feature about the chair. The arms of the chair were not on the side but stretched out high in opposite directions. When a patient was strapped into place, it gave the appearance of a crucifixion.

Their mouths were gagged. This eliminated any distraction from the patient screaming, also cursing, spitting, and of course, biting.

The two guards, who delivered the patient to the room and strapped them in, remained in the room throughout the procedure. Insane people were known to possess great strength. It wasn't uncommon for a patient to break free of their bonds. This proved true for women as well as men.

A sharp lancet was used to open the vein. The trick was to cut the vein without collapsing it. Both arms were used, each time finding a new spot to cut. Multiple cuts in the same wound did not have time to heal, causing possible infection. A porcelain lined metal bowl was held under the arm, catching the flow of blood. It didn't take long; not much was needed.

This blood was taken to the laboratory and placed in vials for later study. The liquid was compared in color and consistency to what they assumed to be healthy blood from a sane person. La Tueur was usually the donor of this blood. The blood was also mixed with other liquids, such as water, vinegar, and bleach, to see how it would respond.

It was an easy task for the guards when it was time to return the patient to their cell. Usually, they went limp, needing to be carried. The ordeal left them weak and vulnerable. They were brought to death's door, only one step short of eternity. Once in their cell, they'd collapse on the bed, sleeping for hours, sometimes all the way through till the next day.

A patient could expect to be bled at least once each week, twice if the doctor thought it necessary. For some reason, Georgette was the exception. Often she was bled four or five times a week.

****

Jolene had no understanding of medical procedure, yet looking at Georgette; she knew something was wrong, each day her condition worsened. Her beautiful full black hair became brittle; her flawless skin grew pale with many sores that never healed. Her eyes were sunken with dark circles around them. She couldn't walk the length of her cell without stumbling, and then falling onto her bed. Conversation was becoming difficult, her mind was slipping.

She seldom slept or ate, making her symptoms worse. Often, Jolene would return to Georgette's cell to retrieve her food tray only to find none of it had been touched.

Without sleep or food, being bled so often, a person could only survive for so long. Georgette was approaching death quickly. If no one helped her, she would be gone within a week.

Eighteen

Till Death Do Us Part

From the day of her first conversation with Georgette, Jolene kept her eyes and ears open. Was the woman telling the truth? Chances were she wasn't. This was an insane asylum. Patients have delusions. Still, there was a ring to Georgette's story that sounded true. Jolene had to know. Only, how, whom could she ask, certainly not La Tueur. She would bide her time, watching and listening.

What made matters worse, her talks with Georgette were clear, to the point conversations. Not the ravings of a madwoman. What else was true, Georgette was being bled twice as often as the other patients. Jolene was no expert; still it was plain to see that Georgette's health was failing. She would not out live the month.

"I tell you I am his wife," Georgette insisted. "There must be proof somewhere." She thought for a moment. "Once I'm dead and gone, he will be entitled to my fortune. Somewhere there is a marriage license to prove this. Then you will believe me."

"I'll try," Jolene said, knowing full well what Georgette asked was a near impossibility.

The next few days, Jolene waited for a chance to inspect the doctor's office. It came one day when La Tueur entered the kitchen, asking for a pot of tea. As always, Jolene brewed up a pot, delivering it on a tray to his office. He must have been called away by one of the guards, the office was empty.

Jolene looked around, frantically. Where should she start? Where would someone hide a piece of paper? The room was filled with papers. Those scattered on his desk, surely couldn't be what she was looking for. No one would leave such an important document lying around. Or is that what you do because you know no one would suspect you of doing so. There were stacks of papers, files on all the patients of Masion de fous. Strangely enough, there was no file on Georgette, nothing.

It must be locked away. Something so important would surely be locked away, only where...in a wall safe? Jolene started looking behind pictures hung on the wall for a safe. Then it dawned on her how useless this was. If she found one, she couldn't open it.

Two walls of the office were bookshelves from floor to ceiling with hundreds of books on them. The document could be hidden between the pages of one of the books. Searching for it would take hours. Jolene only had minutes.

In desperation, Jolene tried the drawers of the desk. They were all locked, except for the right-handed draw at the bottom of the desk. Inside, there were pens and a bottle of ink, sheets of blank writing paper, and a ring of keys. On top of it all was a two-bullet derringer, a small pistol, deadly, nonetheless. She moved the papers aside. Underneath was a small photograph in a decorative frame made of abalone. She lifted it out and up to take a closer look.

It was a wedding picture, a bride and a groom on their wedding day. There was no mistaking it. The groom was Doctor Andre La Tueur and the bride was Georgette.

Just then, the doorknob turned slowly. Jolene tossed the photograph back into the drawer, slamming it shut. In walked La Tueur.

"What are you doing here?" he shouted, his eyes wide and full of fire.

"I brought you your tea, sir," she said shyly.

"What are you doing behind my desk?"

"I was just moving some of your papers to the side. I didn't want them to get tea on them."

"Well, I don't like it. In fact, from now on you never enter my office when I'm not here. You understand?"

"Yes, sir…"

"Now, get out of here."

Jolene rushed from behind the desk, around La Tueur, and out of the office.

****

In time, it became clear Georgette would not live much longer. She needed to escape, if she were to live. She could not do so on her own. It was up to Jolene. She would help her escape; it was the only right thing to do.

Jolene kept a lookout for an opportunity. If she failed, it would be of her own accord, for there was no one she could rely on, and no one she would jeopardize by asking for help. She was on her own. Though she didn't feel alone, her prayers gave her strength and resolve.

It was the end of the week. All the patients had recently been bled. Each of them lay weakened in their cell. Releasing Georgette from her cell would be easy. The master key was attached to a large metal ring that hung on the far wall. It was getting out and away from Masion de fous that was the problem. Without a plan, Jolene moved forward.

There were no guards on the second floor. Jolene took down the key, and opened Georgette's cell. The poor woman was out cold on her bed.

"Wake up, you must wake up," Jolene whispered, standing over her.

Georgette's eyes burst open, her right hand shot up, grabbing Jolene by the throat in a death grip.

Jolene could barely talk; the woman's hand was as strong as a vice.

"Georgette, it's me, Jolene, I've come to set you free."

She let go, Jolene fell to her knees, chocking.

"Where are the guards?" Georgette asked.

"We must be quiet," Jolene warned.

Hearing the noise, a guard came up the stairs to investigate. Georgette hid to one side. When the guard passed, she took him from behind, wrapping her arm around his neck in a stranglehold. The man's eyes bulged from his head, as he was cut off from precious air, his life slowly leaving him.

"Stop it, you're killing him!" Jolene pleaded.

It seemed impossible that a woman who was so close to death could muster up so much strength. The man's eyes rolled back in his head, she let him go to fall to the floor, dead.

"Georgette, listen to me," Jolene begged.

Georgette seemed to not hear a word. There was a lit hurricane lamp hanging on the wall, she took hold of it, and started down the stairs, followed closely by Jolene.

Strangely enough, Georgette knew her way around the first floor. She went directly to La Tueur's office. There, she kicked in the door.

La Tueur sat behind his desk. When the door burst open, he jumped to his feet. The look of surprise in his eyes told the true story. Georgette, his wife was the last person he expected to see. Fear washed over his face.

"You didn't even have the decency to kill me straight out," Georgette said. "No, you had to torture me, killing me slowly, a little each day. What for? You did it for money to buy all this, your own personal kingdom? You lied to me! You never even loved me."

"This woman is insane," La Tueur shouted, pointing at Georgette. "She has delusions. She thinks she's my wife."

"That's a lie!" Jolene cried. "I saw the wedding photograph!"

Just then they heard the stirring of footsteps rushing toward them.

"Georgette, let's go, the guards are coming," Jolene warned.

Quickly she turned, pushing Jolene out of the room, slamming the door. Jolene heard the lock turn.

"Georgette…!" Jolene shouted.

Large hands grabbed Jolene by the shoulders, pushing her aside.

"Open up!" one of the guards demanded. He pounded on the door again and again. Finally, he gave up, stepping out of the way. "Bust it down," he ordered the other guards. They slammed into the door with their shoulders, putting all their weight and strength behind it.

Meanwhile, inside the drama was unfolding.

"When I realized you didn't really love me, I wanted to die," Georgette confessed. "I still feel that way. Only, I'll be dammed if I give you the satisfaction of living on after me. Till death do us part, my dear husband."

"You're insane," La Tueur growled.

"You should know, my darling, you made me this way."

The next instant, La Tueur quickly opened the right hand drawer of his desk, pulling out the derringer. He aimed the weapon at his wife, pulling the trigger. The bullet hit Georgette square in the chest, into her heart. Blood sprouted forward. The same moment, she hurled the hurricane lamp at her husband. It hit him in the chest, shattering. In the blink of an eye, he burst into flames. He hollered in pain, a human torch rushing for the door.

Georgette threw her arms around him. They fell to the floor, together. With the last of her strength and will she held him tightly in her embrace. The next moment, they were both in flames.

When the guards finally bashed open the door, it was too late. The entire office was engulfed. All those books and papers made it a tinderbox.

"Let's get out of here!" one of the guards shouted, turning and running. The other guards did the same.

"What about the patients?" Jolene called to them, watching them flee out the front door.

It didn't take long for the fire to spread through the building. Smoke was everywhere, getting thicker by the minute.

Jolene rushed upstairs to Georgette's cell to find the master key. When she found it, she went from cell to cell opening the door.

"Fire…fire…save yourself!" Jolene shouted.

In many cases, it was useless. The patient wouldn't leave, no matter how Jolene pleaded with them; they remained staring at the walls of their cell. There were two or three who fled to the stairs, save for them most remained.

When she opened the last cell door, a squatty little man with monstrously strong arms ran out at her. He grabbed Jolene, tossing her about like a sack of rags. She tried to fight him, except his insane strength was too much for her. Lastly, he tossed her into the wall, hitting the back of her head. She fell unconscious to the floor.

When she came to, smoke was all she could see. She made her way to the stairs strictly by memory. The entire first floor was on fire. Flames shot up the stairs at her, blocking her passage.

She remembered there was a water bucket the guards kept on hand against the wall. She felt around till she found it. It was full. She lifted it about her head, dousing herself.

She rushed down the stairs, covering her face with her arms. Downstairs was like a furnace. She had to move fast, the heat was intense. There was so little air to breath; she got down as close to the floor as she could. Again, she moved about by memory only. In her confusion, she could have been moving in the wrong direction.

She made it to the hallway. Rushing forward, she saw the front door. Waves of heat blinded her. She made it to the exit. The brass doorknob was like a hot coal, burning her hand as she turned it.

When the door opened, the air rushed into the house to the hungry flames. Stepping outside was when she realized her dress was on fire.

The fire shot up along her side. She ran in terror. The more she ran, the more the air fed the flames.

Philippe ran after her, tackling her to the ground. He rolled her around on the lawn till the fire was out. Much of her dress was burned, other than that she was unharmed, thankfully. Once again, Philippe saved her life.

He carried her, placing her down under a tree, a far distance from the burning building. Gabrielle lifted Jolene's head, giving her a drink of water.

"Are ya all right?" Gabrielle asked.

"I think so."

By now, the building was a massive orange glow, lighting up the sky. The entire area was bathed in light. Long shadows danced with the flicker of the flames.

"How many got out?" Jolene asked.

"Don't rightly know, yet," Philippe said.

"Did ya see the doctor?" Gabrielle asked Jolene.

She didn't know what to say. The full answer was so complicated. So, she told as much as she felt would suffice.

"He's dead," Jolene whispered.

"Well, that truly is the end of Masion de fous," Gabrielle said. "Guess we better start lookin' for a place to go," she said to Philippe.

"I've got to go. I can't stay," Jolene declared

"Where ya gonna go?"

"I don't know, but I can't stay here. Do a favor for me?"

"What's that?"

"If anybody asks, you never knew anyone named Jolene. I was never here."

"Why?"

"It's a long story, something in my past."

Gabrielle smiled. "Girl, we all got a past, and those always seem to be the longest stories. Don't ya worry, I won't tell a soul."

Jolene stood up; she hugged Gabrielle and Philippe good-bye. There was so much confusion around, she moved about unnoticed.

Luckily, the front gate was unguarded. She slipped through, looked back one more time, turned and walked out of the light of the fire, away from Masion de fous, disappearing into the night.

Nineteen

I Feel Naked

Jolene was a sight, walking along the road going south. She was unwashed and unkempt, her clothes torn and singed. She prayed as she walked. She prayed for forgiveness. Her heart was full of dismay at all she had experienced since being on her own. Sometimes, she felt so down in herself, she wanted to give up. This was wrong and she knew it.

"Dear Father in heaven, please, forgive me. Wash away this feeling of despair; fill my heart with thy joy."

Her prayers were answered. She traveled onward with newfound faith and reassurance in the future. With God's help, she would not only survive but prevail.

A few miles north of New Orleans, she came upon a roadside inn. It was a two-story building, rooms for rent on the second floor; the first floor was a combination, tavern and restaurant. It offered everything a traveler on their way to and from New Orleans could want. The owner and proprietor lived with his wife in a small shack around back, next to a large barn.

Jolene went around back to the kitchen. She knocked on the door.

A rotund little man with a ruddy face answered. "What do you want?" he asked coldly.

"Please, sir, I haven't eaten in days. Could you spare something to eat?"

He pointed to an area behind her.

"You see that pile of wood; you see that axe. You cut that wood up for the stove; I'll give you a meal." He slammed the door in her face.

It was slow going. Jolene had never wheeled an axe before. Even at her healthiest, she was never that strong. It took her longer than it should have; in time she finished. She returned to the backdoor.

"I finished," she told the man when he answered her knock.

"Wait here," was all he said, closing the door.

A few minutes later, he appeared. He handed her a plate.

"You can sit on the steps and eat. Knock when you're done."

There was one fried egg, an overcooked piece of bacon, and a slice of bread. When she finished, she knocked on the door. The man came out, taking the plate from her. His wife stood behind him. She was a round little woman, a female version of her husband in a dress.

"I could use some help," said the woman to her husband.

"I'll give you three meals a day. You can sleep in the barn," he said.

To Jolene, it sounded like paradise. She nodded.

For the rest of the day, they kept her busy with cleaning the kitchen, the tavern, and the upstairs rooms. By the end of the day, she lay on a pile of hay in the barn. She felt exhausted, however, she now had a place to sleep and her stomach was full.

****

Days turned into weeks, weeks into months. Nothing changed. She labored the whole day long, ate her meals, slept in the barn. She spoke with no one. In all that time, she never even learned the names of her employers. Only orders were spoken to her. They didn't treat her cruelly, just with indifference. The good thing was she was feeling well and strong, and knowing she could leave anytime she wanted, no questions asked.

One afternoon, Jolene was out back washing bedsheets in a large tub. An old black man came hobbling over to her. His bent back could only be from a lifetime of working in the cotton fields.

"I was told to give ya this," he said, handing her a folded slip of paper.

Jolene opened and read it.

I have done you a disservice. Let me make it up to you.

"Who gave you this?" Jolene asked.

"Some black woman, dark skinned, very pretty, dressed fine, too. She gave me a whole dollar to give it to ya."

"You don't know her name?"

"I ain't never seen her before."

The old man turned, walking away.

"Thank you," Jolene called to him.

He continued walking, waving back over his shoulder.

There was an address at the bottom of the piece of paper – *169 St. Charles Avenue.*

That night in the barn, she thought long and hard. What black woman had ever offended her? No one came to mind. She decided the next day she would find out.

****

It was a three-story building in one of the finer neighborhoods of New Orleans, a tall, slender structure. Walking up the steps to the front door, before she could knock it opened. A very lovely, young black woman greeted her with a smile. She was dressed in the height of fashion. Jolene did not recall ever meeting her.

"You must be Jolene. We've been expecting you," she said, moving aside, allowing Jolene to enter.

"What's this all about?" Jolene asked. "Who are you?"

"My name's not important. I was the one who got the letter to you. However, you're not here to see me. Don't worry it will all make sense in time. Follow me. This is your lucky day."

Jolene was very skeptical, not believing in luck. As they passed the parlor, Jolene looked in. It was a room full of finery. What caught her eye was there were three other black women lounging about. They were all as beautiful and well-dressed as her escort.

"Are they Fancy Ladies?" Jolene asked.

The woman laughed, "It's something like that, only better."

Her answer made no sense to Jolene.

Jolene followed her up the stairs and down a hallway. They entered a room. It was a bedroom, spacious, done up for a woman of quality.

"This will be your room," she announced, walking over to a closet. "These are your clothes."

"I don't understand," Jolene said.

"Trust me, I told you it's your lucky day. Why don't you get out of those filthy rags, get yourself cleaned up, and get dressed. I'll be back for you in an hour."

With that she left the room. Alone, Jolene eyed the dresses. She'd never seen so many beautiful clothes. None of it made any sense. Still, if someone wanted to do her any harm, they would have already done it.

Later, the woman entered the room without knocking.

"Well, are you ready?"

"Ready, for what…?" Jolene asked, sounding a bit dismayed.

She just smiled, leading Jolene back into the hall. They walked up the stairs to the third floor. There was only one door. The woman knocked.

"Come in," a man's voice came through the door.

The woman opened the door, pushed Jolene inside, slamming the door behind her.

The entire third floor was one immense apartment, with a sleeping area to one side, a fully stocked bar to the far wall, a library in one corner, and fireplaces at both ends. In the center of the room was what could only be described as a sitting room. Everything about it said *Great Wealth*.

In the heart of it all, standing facing her was the last man she ever expected to see. There, dressed in the height of fashion, looking as handsome as ever, was Graham Dorsey. He stood before her smiling, her greatest love, her biggest disappointment, and most memorable betrayal.

Her knees went weak. She wanted to say something, only nothing came out of her mouth.

"Jolene, it's so good to see you, again. I've never stopped thinking about you. I feel bad about the way we parted."

"I do, too," Jolene said, not meaning it in the same way as he.

"As you can see, life has been good to me," he said, pointing out the features of the massive room. "How have you been?"

Jolene sighed deep and loud. "What is it, Graham? What do you want?"

"Now, Jolene, don't be like that. It's all water under the bridge. Let bygones be bygones."

She remained staring at him, coldly. There was a storm brewing within her. She was angry, mad, disgusted, and still in love with him. Even though she knew how foolish that was. She'd hide it, never giving him the satisfaction. Finally, she spoke, "You robbed me of more things than I could count. I prayed for your soul, often."

She was about to turn and leave.

"No, wait," he beseeched her. "I'm sorry; let me make it up to you."

He stepped toward her. Taking an envelope from his jacket, he handed it to her.

"What is this?" she asked, looking at the packet in her hand.

"It's not much; still it's the least I can do."

Jolene opened it. There was a wad of cash in it. She didn't bother to count it, throwing it at his feet.

"You think I'm so easily bought?"

"I see you're angry. I don't blame you, Jolene. Let me make it up to you. Stay here with me; I'll make it up to you."

"What, and be one of your Fancy Girls?" she said in a chilling tone, pointing to the door, indicating she knew of the women in his harem.

He chuckled slightly, "I have to confess, I do like the colored girls."

"Well, I will never be one."

He grew serious, "If that's the way you want it, then so be it. But we can still do some good for each other." He walked over to the far wall, taking down a bottle of whiskey. "Would you like a drink?" Then he thought about what he'd said. "Oh, that's right, saints don't drink. They don't drink, they don't steal, they don't lie, and they have no taste for carnal pleasure. Well, I do." He poured himself a whiskey. "I'll make you a proposition. Stay here, work for me. I promise you will not be molested. You will not have to do anything against that high moral code of yours. All I want is that sweet, innocent looking, angelic face of yours to greet my business associates. All you'll need to do is smile, look pretty, and serve drinks and sandwiches. I need you to be a hostess, that's all. Please, say yes."

"I'll think about it," she answered.

Graham bent down, picked up the envelope filled with money, and handed it to her. "Please, take this, don't refuse me. It will never repay you for the wrong I've done you, but it would make me feel relieved if you did."

"I said I'd think about it."

He smiled, "Go back to your room. There's a satin chord on the wall near the bed. Pull it. Someone from the kitchen will come; have them make you something to eat. Rest, make yourself at home. Think about it."

Then he did something she least expected. He leaned forward, kissing her cheek. She should have slapped him. She should have turned and left the house, back to the streets. Instead, the scent of him made her swoon.

"Think about it," he whispered. "But say yes."

****

For the next two weeks, Rosiline, the beautiful young woman who greeted Jolene when she first arrived, tutored her in the ways of being a good hostess. The purpose was to help with the service during Graham's nightly card games. It was in this manner he had become so wealthy. He had a way with cards and gambling. He seldom lost. Often, he was accused of cheating, except no one ever could say how.

The other women who lived under Graham's roof could have easily hosted. They were smart enough, well-groomed, and beautiful. Still, Graham insisted Jolene had a quality they hadn't, a look of innocence, he believed the men who'd come to gamble would appreciate. "It will put them at ease," Graham often said.

Jolene was treated well, though she spent most of her time alone. She had little to no contact with the other women, except Rosiline, who though friendly, was not familiar. She never showed any interest in having a relationship with anyone, least of all Jolene.

Rosiline spent hours with Jolene, teaching her the skills of being a good hostess. She taught Jolene the different whiskeys. They all looked the same to Jolene. Rosiline showed her how to pour and how to serve.

Then there were the foods, how to plate and serve them. She demonstrated how to cut meat and cheese for sandwiches, which were numerous. The bread needed to be sliced thin, the ingredients placed or spread on in the proper order and amount. Always start by buttering the bread, never cut the crust unless asked to. Available ingredients were onion, lettuce, parsley, olives, chopped pickles, hard-boiled eggs, ham, salmon, anchovies, mashed beans, and a large variety of cheeses.

The night Jolene was to begin, Rosiline came to her room, holding up a gown to Jolene. It was green satin with fine white lace.

"It's beautiful," Jolene proclaimed," However, it's a little too revealing, don't you think?"

"Graham insists you wear it, tonight."

Rosiline helped Jolene put it on. Looking at her image in the mirror, she was sure it was too much exposure for her modest nature. Her shoulders were completely uncovered. The back low-cut, the front revealing more cleavage than Jolene felt comfortable showing.

"You look like a princess!" Rosiline declared.

"Maybe so, but I'm freezing."

The two women fell into each others arms, laughing.

The third floor apartment was where it was to be held. Rosiline left her to enter, alone. None of the guest had arrived yet. Graham stood to greet her. Jolene entered, shyly trying to cover herself by crossing her arms.

"You look fabulous," he proclaimed.

"I feel naked," Jolene said.

"That's because the most essential part of your costume is missing," he said, walking toward her, holding up a necklace to her. He got behind her, attaching it around her neck. It was a thick gold weave with pearls imbedded in it every two inches. In the center was a large red ruby, the size of her fist.

"Now, you are complete," he decreed "Go to your post, and make yourself ready."

Soon the guests arrived, men of various ages, all of them clearly wealthy. There were five of them, Graham made six. They sat at a round table in the middle of the room. Jolene took their drink orders – whiskey all around.

"Graham, I always have a big thirst, why do you insist on us drinking out of these tiny glasses?" asked one of the men.

"They're more refined" Graham answered. "Don't worry, my girl will fill it up as often as you like."

"Who is this new girl?" another asked. "She's easy on the eyes. How much...?"

"She's not for sale or hire," Graham responded.

The man laughed, "You haven't heard my price, yet."

"Let's see if you can afford anything, by the end of the night," Graham said, smiling, yet serious.

It was true, all nightlong; Jolene was constantly moving from man to man, pouring whiskey. Larger glasses would have made her job easier. That's not to mention how much they ate. She served plate after plate of food, and then would scurry for the whiskey bottle, frantically rushing around the table, pouring as fast as they could lift their glasses.

At midnight, it didn't look like any of them had any intentions of calling it a day. They were just getting started. Graham was the big winner. He wanted to continue, while his lucky streak lasted. The others wanted to continue because Graham won so much and so often. They believed his luck couldn't last, and they'd be able to win back some, if not all of their money, perhaps even get ahead.

As always when Graham was winning, someone would make a comment, jokingly at first. "How do you do it, Graham?"

"It's skill, my friend."

"So you say."

"Are you implying something?"

"Me, no, I don't imply anything, not without proof, I don't. But if I ever learn that you've cheated me, I won't just imply." He laid his hand down, looking Graham straight in the eye. "I'll kill you."

The two men laughed it off, continuing their play.

Two hours later, Graham was still the winner; Jolene was still frantically pouring whiskey into those little glasses. Understandably, Jolene was a beautiful young girl; all eyes were on her as she moved, all except one. His name was Tom Courtney, after a time of loosing so much money, his eyes focused on Graham. If he was cheating, Tom wanted to catch him.

Jolene remained busy, fluttering about the table, serving drinks. As she moved about, all eyes followed. It was then Tom Courtney became suspicious. Perhaps Graham was using her beauty as a distraction. From then on, instead of watching Jolene, he watched Graham. For the life of him, he couldn't see any cheating.

Believing the game was on the up and up, Tom resumed to ogling Jolene, along with the other men. That's when he saw it. How Graham had been cheating them. Graham knew what cards the others held in their hands because of Jolene.

It was just a chance glance; Tom looked at the ruby in the center of her necklace. Within it, Tom saw the hand of the man she was serving whiskey to.

When she came around to serve him his drink, he reached out, ripping the necklace from her neck.

"What is this?" he exclaimed to all, turning the gem around, exposing the backside. It was covered with a thin layer of paint, as a mirror would be. Graham knew everyone's holdings by the reflection in that oversized ruby.

Realizing he'd been caught, that a conflict was unavoidable, Graham jumped from his seat, tossing the chair aside, he backed away. Only it was too late, Tom Courtney, rose from his chair, drew his pistol, shooting Graham.

The gun blast was earsplitting and powerful. Hitting him square in the chest, the force lifted him off his feet, sending him backwards, and flying through the window. There was the sound of the glass shattering. As Graham fell down out of sight, they could hear screaming, ending with a thunderous thud when he hit the ground.

Tom pointed the gun at Jolene. "And now for you, missy…"

"I had nothing to do with it, gentlemen. I didn't know. I swear," Jolene begged.

"Leave the girl alone, Tom," said one of the other men. "The authorities will be here soon. We all know you were in the right, but I don't want to spend the next four to five hours explaining what happened."

With that, the men rushed out of the apartment. Jolene stood for a moment, in deep shock. When she came to her senses, she knew it would be foolish to remain. She had to run away.

Downstairs in her room, she undressed. A gown would be too cumbersome, and too memorable. Once in a more presentable dress, she reached up to the top rung in her closet. She took down the envelope containing the money Graham gave her. The next instant, she was hit on the side of the head, landing on the floor; the envelope fell from her hand.

It was two of the other women, two of Graham's Fancy Ladies. Neither one of them was Rosiline. They laughed, as they seized the envelope, and ran out the room, and out of the house.

Once Jolene regained her bearings, she jumped to her feet, ran down the stairs and out the door.

She couldn't help stop for a moment outside the house to look at Graham. Sprawled out on the pavement was the only man she had ever loved. His chest opened wide from the bullet blast, the back of his head split open, oozing like a cracked egg all over the pavement, down to the gutter.

She felt sad, heartbroken, yet most of all, she felt sorry for him. She would have prayed over him, only there was no time. She heard voices shouting off in the distance, coming closer.

Wiping the tears from her eyes, she turned, running off into the night.

Twenty

The Hanging Game

It was late, the streets were dark, still Jolene moved about in the shadows. About a quarter mile from where she started, she turned the corner to see two rough young men beating up on a well-dressed older gentleman. It didn't take them long to incapacitate the old man, taking his purse from him, and then running off.

Jolene fell to her knees. She turned the old man over, instantly recognizing him. He was one of the gamblers at the card games held at Graham Dorsey's home, that very night.

"Are you all right, sir?" she asked turning him over.

"I wish I was young, again, just once. I'd show those ruffians a thing or two."

He recognized her, as well. Though for the life of him he couldn't remember from where. She was wearing a different dress than when he saw her. As well, he was badly shaken. Once he stood up, he took stock of himself.

"They took my wallet. What does it matter? There couldn't have been more than one hundred dollars in it."

A person has to be very wealthy to dismiss one hundred dollars so easily.

"Do you recognize me?" Jolene asked.

"Why, do I know you? You look familiar."

"I was at the card game, just now; I was the one serving the drinks and food."

"Oh, was that you? Sad, about Graham, it was a bad deal, all the way around."

"My name is Jolene Fairchild."

"I'm Derwood Sullivan. My friends call me Sully. You may call me Sully."

"Can I walk you home, Sully?"

"If you like, it's not far ahead."

As they walked on, Jolene questioned him.

"I know we don't really know each other, but after what happened tonight, I'm jobless and homeless. There isn't any place you know that I might find one or both?"

"My dear, you can sleep the night on my kitchen floor, except you must be gone by the morning. As for work, I have a full staff at my home. I do have one suggestion, only I don't know if it will agree with you."

"I'm willing to do anything," Jolene answered.

"I own a factory on the waterfront. It's called the Black Betty Blacking Company. We manufacture boot polish. I own it, yet I know little about it. I have a manager who runs it for me. I visit it only once a month, for no reason other than habit, I don't know. As long as it puts money in the bank, why make waves, I always say. Well, I do know they're always looking for workers. It's a difficult job, and not a very nice place, from what I gather."

"I need work, sir; I'd appreciate any help I can get."

"Very well, sleep on the kitchen floor; I'll bring you there first thing in the morning."

Sully guided her to a home larger and grander than Graham's. Before he could unlock the front door, his manservant opened it.

"I will see you in the morning," Sully assured her.

The manservant took her to the kitchen, got her a blanket, leaving her without saying a word. Jolene made the best of it, wrapping the blanket around her, sleeping on the floor.

****

She didn't get much sleep. She was roused early by the clatter of the kitchen help preparing breakfast.

Sully came in, dressed for the day, and ready.

"See that this girl is well-fed," he told his staff. "I'll be back for you after you've eaten," he told Jolene.

An hour later, Sully was guiding her down a street toward the harbor. They stopped in front of a large brick warehouse. It was a sad and dingy building; all the windows were blacked out.

"I told you it wasn't a nice place," Sully said. "Then again, any port in a storm, as they say. You can work here till you get on your feet, again."

Two armed guards answered the door. Inside, it was darker than one would imagine. They sent for the manager.

His name was Rueland, a large white man, both tall and wide. His arms and shoulders were massive, covered with a coat of thick black hair. The curls on his head were black, as well; his unkempt beard was the same, covering up a seriously bad complexion of pot marks and redness. His dark eyes were close and set deep, shadowed by his thick eyebrows. His grooming and dress was in the manner of a man who never took pride in himself, or cared what others thought. His body odor was so strong and polluted; one need only be within a few feet of him to catch the foulness of him.

"Mr. Sullivan, how time flies. Is it the end of the month, already?"

"Oh, no," laughed Sully. "I've brought you a new worker for the factory."

"We will put her to good use," Rueland said.

"Best of luck, dear girl, I will be back at the end of the month to look in on you," Sully said before leaving.

The metal door slammed like a prison cell. The guards locked it, and stood in front of it, again.

Jolene stepped forward, smiling. "My name is..."

Before she could finish, Rueland gave her the back of his hand, sending her flying backward and to the floor.

"You, stupid girl, there's no talking here, only work. Put her to work," he ordered one of the guards.

Within minutes, Jolene was sitting at a long table with a long line of other women, white and black, pasting labels on the finished containers of blacking. Looking around at the faces of the other women, it was obvious Jolene was once again in the worst of places.

They worked in silence. If any of them spoke, the guards would whip them. The picture on the label was a cartoon face of a little black child, she smiled from ear to ear, and her hair done up in pigtails. On it was written: *Black Betty Blacking – The best money can buy*.

The work was not hard; still the tediousness of having to repeat the same action, never slowing down or the guards would beat you, was torture.

There was a foul odor in the air that could not be described. Cooking the ingredients for the blacking in a large vat gave off fumes that filled the entire building. It made your eyes tear; burned your throat and lungs, where it would settle like hot tar.

At the end of the day everyone working in the different departments was gathered into a large hall with long tables and benches. There, they were fed a meager meal of stew and bread.

Looking around, Jolene saw no men other than the guards that were numerous and everywhere you looked. All the workers were women of various ages, from ten-year-old girls to elderly women. During supper, again, if anyone so much as whispered, they were whipped.

Afterwards, they were led to long rooms with single cots lining both sides of the room. Jolene was assigned a bed.

In the dark, Jolene, as tired as she was, found it difficult to sleep. She looked to the bed next to hers. On it lay the prettiest, dark-haired, white girl, perhaps a year or two younger than Jolene. Her eyes were wide, welled up with sorrow.

"What is your name?" Jolene whispered.

"Bernadette," the girl said in a low voice.

"How long have you been here?"

"I don't remember. I only know it's been a very long time."

Then Jolene asked the question that was heavy on her heart, "Does anyone ever get out of here?"

"No," Bernadette replied. "They work you to death. Everyday more girls are brought, while many die and are carted away. You will see. In the morning, at least two or three of these women will die in their sleep."

"Shut up, and get to sleep!" one of the guards shouted.

Bernadette went silent, turning over in her cot.

Jolene prayed in her mind, "Oh Lord, is this the fate of your children who try to do what's right?" Then a wave of shame washed over her. "Oh Lord, forgive me. Teach me to be humble and grateful to appreciate all the blessings heaven allows."

****

As the days passed, they became darker; hopelessness abound. Jolene got to work in the different departments, from stoking the fire under the vat, to pouring and canning, storing and packing, and then back to gluing on labels.

Against regulations, Jolene and Bernadette would whisper for hours during the night. They got to know each other well, becoming close friends.

Bernadette's story was a sad one. She was the youngest of seven children. Her parents were sharecroppers. When money became short and the bills were due, in desperation, her father sold her to Rueland. The best she could figure was it had been at least a year since she arrived.

One night, Jolene was woken from a deep sleep by one of the guards.

"Come with me," he whispered softly.

She'd learn better than to question. She followed him down a long corridor, and down a flight of stone stairs, she didn't even know existed. At the bottom was a large metal door.

"Go on," said the guard, turning, climbing up, leaving her.

She opened the door and entered. It was a dark room with walls of stone with thick wooden beams running the length of the small room. She jumped back in fright when she saw Rueland. He was standing in the middle of the room, stark naked, holding a whip in one hand and a pistol in the other.

"Come in, my child," Rueland laughed.

There was nothing in the room, save for a large armchair and a three-legged stool. The stool was in the center of the room, underneath one of the wooden beams, from the beam hung a thick hemp rope that was tied off to another beam. The other end of the rope that dangled above the three-legged stool was tied in a hangman's noose.

Understanding there was no good to come of this Jolene fell to her knees before him. "Oh, please, sir, have pity on me. Please, don't let me do this. It is a sin. I will do anything, but not that. Kneel with me and pray for forgiveness."

"God…!" Rueland shouted. "How I do love it when they beg." He began whipping her. "Take off your clothes!"

Realizing her innocents and pleading only inflamed his passion the more, Jolene disrobed, covering herself with her hands as best she could.

"Stand on the stool," he commanded.

Jolene stood atop the stool. He reached up, placing the hangman's noose around her neck. Under the armchair was a sickle, the kind used for cutting wheat in the fields. He took it up, handing it to Jolene. He sat down in the armchair, pointing the pistol at her heart.

He held the gun in one hand, in the other was a cord. The other end of the cord was tied to one of the legs of the stool.

"Look at me. Don't take your eyes off me. Don't even blink," he stated in a very serious tone. "I'm going to pull the stool out from under you. You will hang from the rope by your neck. You have the sickle. You can cut yourself free anytime you wish. But if you cut yourself down before I am satisfied, I will shoot you. Keep your eyes on me."

He made the cord connected to the stool taunt. He played and teased her, falsely tugging on the cord, yet not hard enough to remove the stool. Each time he did this, Jolene's heart jumped into her throat. She held onto the sickle, ready to cut herself free at a moment's notice.

Jolene was shocked to see how this game of cat and mouse aroused him. Then, without warning, he pulled the stool out from under her. Immediately, she fell down, the rope dug into her neck, cutting off her air. She looked at him; it was difficult to tell if the time was right to cut herself down. Each passing moment stole a bit more of her life. Suddenly, his head went back, as did his eyes in his head. He was in bliss, his personal Nirvana.

Thinking it the right time, Jolene swung the sickle, cutting herself down. She lay on the floor, gasping for breath.

It took a moment for them both to collect themselves.

"Get dressed and get out of my sight," he said, slurring his words.

Not wanting to delay, Jolene took her clothes, and dressed.

"Get out of my sight," Rueland said, again.

Somehow Jolene made it back to her cot.

"Are you all right?" Bernadette asked.

"Yes, I suppose so. It was the most strangest…"

"I know," Bernadette interrupted. "Every woman he finds attractive goes through it. Some men are drawn to this and that. Rueland is drawn to the most evil of thoughts."

Jolene closed her eyes. She fell asleep, praying for the soul of Rueland.

Twenty-One

Something Different

The months passed. Jolene watched women come and go. Many weren't strong enough to withstand such a life. Some broke down mentally. They'd walk about, doing their job in a state that could only be described as near death. Sadly, there were some, a large number to be exact, who committed suicide. Any sharp item would do, a minute when the guards weren't watching. Of course, there were many who just stopped breathing in the middle of the night. It didn't matter to the guards, new women came everyday. There seemed to be an endless supply.

As cruel and miserable as were these women's lives, it was the pretty girls that suffered most. The guards would take them whenever and wherever they wanted. The other women would look the other way, doing their best to block out the screams.

There was a handful of women who were never touched by the guards. They were the ones selected by Rueland for his personal pleasure, each night in the room below – his hanging game. It was a small group of a dozen women, of which Bernadette and Jolene were members.

One day while working the line, gluing labels onto the containers, Jolene heard a familiar voice. She turned to see Rueland walking toward her, accompanied by Sully.

"So how is our little lady doing?" Sully asked, smiling at Jolene.

"Just fine, Mr. Sullivan. She's one of my favorite girls," Rueland replied. Only Jolene knew the truth behind the statement, "One of my favorite girls", had nothing to do with her working ability.

"My goodness," Sully remarked. "You've grown so thin, child." He turned to Rueland. "Is she eating?"

"Like a horse, sir," Rueland said with pride.

"Are you happy with us, my dear?" the old man asked, clearly concerned, not knowing what was taking place in his own establishment.

One look over Sully's shoulder, into Rueland's eyes, Jolene understood how she should answer. "Just fine, sir, thank you very much."

"Well, Rueland, let's go to the office and look over the books."

"It's been a good month, sir."

"Good…good…that's what I like to hear."

"Mr. Sullivan, Mr. Sullivan, sir…" one of the women working the line jumped to her feet, running toward the old man.

"Please, Mr. Sullivan…"

Before she got within ten feet, one of the guards grabbed hold of her from behind, covering her mouth with his hand.

The old man wasn't deaf; however he was hard-of-hearing. He heard nothing of the woman's cries over the dim of the other workers. He and Rueland continued walking to the office. Rueland smiled, nodding over his shoulder to the guard holding the woman. The look was a direct order as to what to do. The guard toted the woman away. No one complained. They put their heads down, continuing their work.

That night when they settled into their cots, the bed that was usually occupied by the woman they took away was empty. The next night there was another woman sleeping there, a new young woman who cried all nightlong. None of the other women reprimanded her. They understood what she was going through. They let her have her moment.

****

At least one night a week, Jolene was summand to the small room at the lower level. There she would be Rueland's unwilling participant in his hanging game. She spoke not a word, knowing it was useless, and might even get her killed. She got through the ordeal by praying silently the entire time for herself, the other women, and for the soul of Rueland.

After many months, one night Jolene was summand to the lower room. Upon entering, it surprised her to see things were slightly different. As always, Rueland stood naked by his armchair, holding his whip and pistol. Only now, they were not alone. Bernadette was there also, and there were two stools and nooses dangling from the overhead beam, instead of the usual one.

"Strip," he said, calmly.

Both Jolene and Bernadette knew better than to argue the point. Disobedience meant at least a whipping, or worse, a bullet to the head. They quietly disrobed.

128

Once they were naked, Rueland made his plans known. "We're going to try something different. The more the merrier, I always say. Get up on the stools, and put the nooses around your necks."

When they were in place, he handed each of them a long, sharp sickle, sitting in his armchair, never taking the aim of his pistol off them.

"You both know the game," he announced. "Tonight we play it with a slight variation." There were two cords, one tied to each of the front leg of their stool. He held both cords in one hand. "I will pull the stools out from under you both at the same time. Of course this will be at my discretion. As always, if you cut your rope before I feel satisfaction, I will shoot you, a quick and merciful death. Now, here is the variation. Once I pull away the stools, and you are both dangling there, the first person to cut themselves down will be killed. It'll be a test of endurance," he laughed.

Fear blared on the faces of Jolene and Bernadette. The two women looked sorrowfully into each other's eyes.

"You do understand?" he said, and then laughing all the louder. "What a foolish question. Who cares if you understand or not? Now, brace yourselves. Make ready, and go!"

He tugged on both cords, only hard enough to move the stools but only a few inches. The two women stiffened, making ready for the jolt. He did these false moves a few times. It seemed to excite him.

Suddenly, he gave the cords a long hard pull. The stools flew out from under them. They both hanged there, swaying and choking. Rueland took aim, first at Jolene, then at Bernadette, and then back. Back and forth he aimed, till he was overcome with ecstasy, a total state of bliss. His eyes rolled back in his head, his body stiffened and shook like someone having a seizure. When he was done, he relaxed in his armchair, still aiming at them.

Both women were choking loudly. Death was moments away, only who would be the first to cut loose?

Finally, when she could take no more, when she was at death's door, Bernadette raised her sickle and cut herself free. Before she hit the floor, Rueland shot her in the head. The body fell lifeless at his feet.

Jolene took advantage of the distraction. At that very moment, she cut her own rope. Falling to her feet, she leaped forward, swinging the sickle across Rueland's throat.

He brought his hand up to his throat. It was useless, like trying to hold back the sea with a broom. Blood spurt everywhere. His naked body was covered in red. Some of it even sprayed on Jolene. As he died, his eyes went wide; a look of surprise and then shame came over him. He had been outsmarted by a young black girl. This was a fate far worse than death. He tried to speak, except the blood had accumulated in his throat, all that came out was gurgling sounds. It took a long time for his last breath to leave him.

When he was motionless, Jolene took hold of Rueland's pistol. She dressed, taking one last sad look at Bernadette before she left the room and climbed the stairs.

The hour was late. Mostly everyone was asleep. There were few guards about, making it easy to move through the dark and silent factory.

She walked past the sleeping quarters; all the women were in their cots. A single guard holding a rifle kept watch.

Jolene stubbed her toe; she bit her lip, not to cry out. The night was so quiet, the sound echoed against the walls. The guard came out to investigate. Jolene hid in the shadows. She kept aim on the guard, as he looked around. Jolene had never held a gun before, let alone fired one. She only knew you needed to point at what you were firing at and pull the trigger. She held her breath.

She moved slightly. The guard pointed his rifle into the dark corner where Jolene sat low.

"Who's there?" he shouted.

Jolene wasn't sure what to do. She scurried out of the corner and down the hall. He fired a shot, barely missing her. She heard the bullet soar past her head.

The shot woke everyone. The women were in an uproar, some were crying, others were screaming.

The other guards were out in full force, running in all directions throughout the factory. Keeping to the shadows, Jolene made her way to the entrance of the building. There were two armed men standing guard.

"Go see what's happening," one said to the other. "Go ahead; I can take care of this myself."

The one guard ran off, holding his rifle in front of him. The remaining guard stood at attention, looking back and forth.

Jolene hid behind some crates. Holding the pistol in both hands, she had a good aim at the guard. She could have easily shot him. However, the thought of killing another human being in cold blood was something she knew she couldn't do.

"Step away from the door," she said firmly.

"Who's there?" he replied.

"I have a gun. I don't want to use it. I will if you don't move away from the door."

"I'm moving…don't shoot…I'm moving."

"Drop your gun."

He did as he was told.

Jolene stepped out from behind the crates, keeping her aim on him.

"Move aside," she said, approaching the door.

He moved slightly to one side."

"More," she said.

He moved a little bit more.

When she got to the door, she reached out to open it. In a blink, he took hold of her.

"Over here…over here!" he shouted, warning the others.

Jolene could hear footsteps.

They fought over the gun. He tried to take it from her. In the struggle, the pistol fired, hitting the guard under his chin. He flew, landing on his back.

Jolene opened the door, rushing out into the cold night air. As she ran, she realized she was still holding the gun. She threw it into the shadows.

"Oh, Lord," she cried as she ran. "I try to do your bidding, yet always fail. Do you not think me an old murderer?"

It would be daylight soon, she had to move quickly, leaving New Orleans far behind.

Twenty-Two

We Own You So Much

The dawn approached. The early morning sun peeked over the horizon. Jolene walked along the side of the road, exhausted. She heard the sound of a carriage draw near from behind her. She realized it would be wiser to get off the road, and hide, only she was too tired. She turned to look behind her to see a two-horse carriage coming up fast. It was a private coach, surely belonging to someone of great wealth, from the look of it. The driver was a young black man dressed in a fine uniform; the horses were matching black stallions. The carriage was shiny, black, deep-varnished wood with golden fixtures.

Just as it was about to pass her, it stopped, abruptly, a voice called out, unseen in the darkness of the carriage.

"Do you need a ride?" It was a woman's voice.

Jolene was too weary to think clearly. She knew what she needed to say, except the exact opposite came out, "Yes, I would very much appreciate it, madam."

Jolene got in the cab, sitting across from the woman. Though it was still early, there was not enough light to make out the woman's features clearly, just her form. From what little Jolene could tell, it was a fine lady, by the scent of her perfume, her fine dress, and the manner in which she spoke indicated a woman of elegance.

As the carriage took a turn in the road, the early morning light flashed across the woman's smiling face. Jolene recognized her immediately.

"Dominique!" Jolene cried out in disbelief.

It was Dominique, the once leader of a gang of roadside bandits, thieves and cutthroats.

"Jolene, how have you been, my dear girl?"

"Dominique, I can't believe it's you. How…?"

"How did I become a lady of refinement? It was all achieved by taking the exact opposite path you have taken, my foolish Jolene. Just one look at you and I know you have continued in your pursuit of goodness and moral Godliness. Only such a path would lead you to be the retched creature before me. I, on the other hand, have lied, cheated, thieved, and murdered my way to the top."

"My reward is not of this world," Jolene replied.

"What is so wrong about living well?" Dominique snapped back.

"Nothing, but at what cost?"

"The cost of others," Dominique laughed. "You are so wrong, Jolene."

"If I am wrong," Jolene said softly and calmly, "and there is nothing beyond this world. When I am dead, I will be in my grave regretting nothing. But if I am right, you are looking at an eternity of regret."

Dominique let out a long, loud laugh. "You still amuse me. No wonder why I've always liked you so." Once her laughter died, she spoke solemnly. "You are still part of my gang, like it or not. I could use you. It would be beneficial to both of us. Listen, carefully."

She'd caught Jolene's attention.

"I am now the mistress of a very wealthy plantation owner, to where I am now journeying to. His name is Boniface Martin. He's older than dirt, a white haired, penguin shaped man. My stomach turns with just the thought of him touching me. Nevertheless, one has to make a living. I've tried to influence him to marry me, only then would his death be of any profit to me. In the meantime, he is best kept alive, for however long possible. Only once you see him, you will understand why I think he will die soon, leaving me only enough to buy a new gown.

"He has been a widower for nearly thirty years. He lives with his son, Edmond, who is closer to my age. The man is a mental deficient. They live in this incredible home, you will see. I know for a fact, Boniface hoards most of his money in his apartment. Where, I've never learned. The problem is there is no time to search. The old buzzard never leaves the house, ever. If I could get him out of that house for at least a few hours, I'm sure I could find his hidden fortune. That's where you will be most useful."

"Me, how is that?" Jolene asked.

"I can never get him to leave his home nor so much as step off his property. Oh, he makes a big fuss over me, showering me with gifts and money. He likes to show me off to his friends at parties. Though he won't admit it, his biggest weakness is young black girls, just like you."

Jolene looked at Dominique, stunned.

"Play up to him. Beg him to take you to New Orleans to buy you something, anything, dresses, jewelry, whatever. He will do what you ask, if you do as I tell you."

"Madam, I'm not the type. What makes you think I could?"

"Because, if you don't, I'll hand you over to the authorities, I'm sure they are still looking for you. Listen, Jolene, this is not a real crime. No one will be hurt. All you have to do is manipulate some old man."

"I won't sleep with him," Jolene insisted.

"You won't have to. All you have to do is make him believe that you will. You can wrap him around your little finger, and I'll show you how."

"Very well, I'll do what you ask," Jolene agreed, although inwardly she swore she would look for an opportunity to warn the old man and foil Dominique's plans.

****

"Boniface, my love, I have a surprise for you," Dominique said in a singsong fashion, peering her head into his apartment. It was a large two-story house. The entire second floor was the one-room of Boniface Martin. Everything else was downstairs, where he seldom ventured.

"A surprise…? I love surprises!" he shouted, walking toward her. His tone of voice and mannerisms gave Jolene pause. Either he was an old man who had gone senile, or worse, he always sounded like a child.

Dominique entered, pulling Jolene alongside.

"A Negress… a pretty one, too!" he exclaimed, still in that infant babble.

"Now…now, you know what happens when you get overly excited," Dominique cautioned in motherly fashion.

He was far more grotesque than Dominique let on, and more than Jolene could imagine. This gnome of a man pawed at her, drooling as a dog salivates over his dinner.

"Not now," Dominique advised, as she pushed Jolene back into the hallway. "Let me clean her up, first, and get her into some decent clothes. We'll see you downstairs at supper."

"Oh, goody," Boniface applauded.

Dominique walked out of the apartment, closing the door. She guided Jolene down the stairs.

"Come, we'll go to my room. You can wear some of my things."

"What is wrong with that man?" Jolene questioned.

"He's mad as a hatter."

"Is he dangerous?"

Dominique chuckled. "I not sure, but it wouldn't surprise me."

****

It was a long room with an equally long dinning table. Boniface sat at the head of the table, his son, Edmond, on his right, Dominique at his left, and Jolene seated next to her.

Jolene couldn't help staring at Edmond and wondering. Dominique described him as a "mental deficient", which made her wonder. It was Boniface who seemed to be the mental deficient, if Edmond was worse, what was he like? Although, he at least had the good sense to not speak and prove her right. In fact, he remained silent throughout the meal.

Dominique told the truth. Boniface Martin loved young black women. Every one of his house help was a young black woman, all very pretty. Overseers managed his plantation for him. He never bothered with such things. Of course, he knew they were robbing him whenever they could. He didn't care, he was rich, and money always flowed in.

Boniface couldn't take his eyes off Jolene.

"Soon, my love, soon," Dominique said to him, smiling.

After supper, Dominique and Jolene joined Boniface in his apartment for brandy. Jolene felt scared and awkward. Earlier, Dominique had told Jolene to play up to Boniface, only she never need say a word. Dominique did all the talking. Telling him how much Jolene loved him and wanted him. All the while, making sure his brandy glass was always full whenever he emptied it, which was often. Jolene wondered if she would ever get the chance to warn the old man, and if she did, would he even believer her, or for that matter, comprehend.

When it was clear he was drunk, Dominique took hold of him by his belt, raising him up from his chair, tugging him over to his bed. She sat on the edge of the bed. She undid his belt and unbuttoned his pants. She pulled his trousers down over his hips. Reaching over to the nightstand, she opened the drawer, taking out a syringe with a hypodermic needle at the end.

"Just another moment, my love; everything will be just fine."

She injected him in his hip. He immediately began to go limp. She stood up, maneuvered him about, letting him free-fall onto the bed. He was out cold. She returned the syringe to the nightstand drawer.

"Morphine," was all she said, and all she need say. "Give me your ribbon," Dominique said, pointing to ribbon around Jolene neck. She placed it in Boniface's hand. "Now, tomorrow we'll tell him you spent the night with him. That he enjoyed it to the highest degree, as well as you. He'll believe it too, the old fool. Damn, if it will make the old boy happy, we'll tell him we both spent the night with him."

****

Jolene was grateful to Dominique. For the next few days she kept the old man drunk and drugged. He remained in a constant stupor. She praised Jolene constantly. Thankfully, Jolene had absolutely no contact with him, outside being in his company with Dominique in the room. There were times Dominique spent the night with him, as well as one or two of the other girls in the household. In the morning, he was unaware what happened during the night, or with whom he spent it. Yet, he believed everything Dominique told him. As far as he knew, he'd spent many a night with Jolene, and was madly in love with her.

As thankful as Jolene was to have the pressure taken from off her, she continued to be cautious of Dominique's motives, knowing she never did anything that wasn't for her own benefit. Not ever having a moment alone with Boniface, she never had the chance to warn him of Dominique's plans. She would have to bide her time, waiting for the right moment.

Just as Dominique predicted, Boniface, at her insistence, agreed to take Jolene into New Orleans for a day of shopping. This would be a rare occasion, as it had been years since he stepped off his property, and decades since he'd been to New Orleans.

On the day of the excursion, Dominique made sure everything was in readiness. The carriage waited outside; the driver, a well-dressed slave, sat on top. Boniface and Jolene got in, sitting forward, together. Dominique stood on the porch waving good-bye.

Before they were even off the property, Boniface took a whiskey flask out of his jacket, putting it to his lips, taking a long hard pull. Farther down the road, Jolene decided it was time to take the matter into her own hands and tell Boniface what was afoot.

"Boniface…?"

"Yes, my love?"

"I have to say something. Dominique wanted you to leave today for a reason."

"Of course, she did. It is to shower you with gifts," he said in a drunken trance, like a person talking in their sleep.

"No, Boniface, she wanted you out of the house so she could search your apartment for whatever money you have hidden."

He laughed, "I have no hidden money."

Just then, the carriage came to an abrupt halt. Jolene looked out the carriage to see three men on horseback with their guns drawn – bandits. She immediately recognized them. It was Dog, Nebo, and Peanut – Dominique's gang.

They dismounted. Peanut started for the carriage door. The other two moved out of sight. Without hesitation, there was a gun blast followed by the sound of a loud thud. They'd killed the driver.

Peanut opened the door, smiled at Jolene. "Ya miss me?" he said, laughing.

"Young man, may I help you?" Boniface asked in a daze.

"My...my, Dominique said he was ugly, but I had no idea. Ya have to hand it to her; she is dedicated to her work."

Boniface smiled, handing his whiskey flask to Peanut. "Here you go, young man. It'll put hair on your chest."

"Don't mind if I do," Peanut said, putting the flask to his lips. Then he looked to Jolene. "Don't ya just hate it when they look ya right in the eye?" He aimed his pistol at Boniface. "Hey, old man, look over there," Peanut said, pointing the flask in the direction of the sky on the other side of the carriage. When Boniface looked out the window and up, Peanut shot him in the side of the head. Jolene jumped from her seat, screaming. "Now...now, don't get all like that," Peanut said, pulling her out of the carriage.

They all mounted their horses. Dog reached down, pulling Jolene up onto a position behind him. Jolene wrapped her arms around him, holding on as they galloped up the road, back to the plantation.

***

Back at the house, the three forced Jolene up the stairs to Boniface's apartment. Standing to greet her were Dominique and Edmond.

"We thank you for your cooperation," Edmond said.

"I don't understand?" Jolene said.

He smiled at her, continuing, "My father hadn't been out of the house in years. We used you to get him out, not to search his apartment. He never kept anything of real value in the house. We knew that. We wanted him out of the house to kill him.

"We couldn't kill him in the house. We'd be suspect. Getting shot by bandits is another matter. Tomorrow, when my father doesn't return, I will tell my concern to the overseers. They'll follow the road to New Orleans and find the carriage with my dead father. The authorities will be notified. When asked, the staff will attest that Dominique and I never left the property. You will be the one and only suspect. We owe you so much, I'm sorry it has to go this way, only you do understand?"

Jolene stepped forward, nearly in tears, her hands folded as she pleaded with Edmond. "Please, sir, I am innocent of all wrongdoing. In the name of heaven, don't do this, I promise I won't tell a soul."

"Of course, you'll tell," Dominique interrupted. "You won't lie, you can't lie. You don't even know how."

"Madam, I've done you no wrong. If I am to be condemned, let it be for my sins, only," Jolene pleaded.

"Very well," Dominique said. "I've always had a soft spot for you. We won't kill you. However, we can't let you simply walk away. Peanut, Dog, Nebo, take her."

With that, the three cutthroats took hold of her, pulling her to the door.

"Where are you taking me?" she cried.

"Were all sinners go," Edmond replied. "You've been sentenced to hell."

Jolene looked at him, bewildered.

"Understand, hell is different for each one of us," he continued. "For my father, hell was a world without drink, drugs, and young pretty black girls."

Dominique took it from there, "For you, hell would be a world without God. So, that's where we're sending you, to where there is no God."

"But God is everywhere," Jolene insisted.

"You really believe that?" Dominique laughed. "Where was God when you were sold? Where was he all the times you were violated? When people stole from you your rights, your dignity, even your own flesh, where was your God, then?"

"He is with me always, giving me the strength to endure all my losses. There is nowhere you can send me where He is not."

"Fine," Edmond snickered. "Then you both can go to hell."

Twenty-Three

More like Lazarus

The three horsemen, with Jolene holding on to the back of Peanut, rode south in the direction of New Orleans. On the outskirts of town, they stopped at a walled mansion. Jolene recognized it immediately.

A large property on the edge of town, surrounded by a high stone walls, guards at the gate, encircled with elaborate gardens on all sides, the house was a two-story mansion with dozens of rooms. It was Madam Charbonneau's school for Fancy Girls, from which Jolene escaped so long ago. Now she was to return to the beginning, to the cruelty and revenge of Madam Charbonneau. Dominique and Edmond spoke truly. For Jolene, this would be hell.

Walking passed the guards, Peanut, Dog, and Nebo delivered her to the front door, and no further, as they were instructed. A maid answered the door, nodding and motioning for Jolene to enter.

"Best of luck, dear heart," Peanut said, taking hold of Jolene's arm, stopping her for a moment. "We were given strict orders to deliver you here, unmolested. Normally, I don't follow orders. Be thankful I value money the highest priority, even above my hankerings. The only constellation I have is knowing how much you've suffered, and knowing that it is only truly beginning." He laughed as they walked away.

Without speaking, the maid brought Jolene to Madam Charbonneau's office, slamming the door behind her once Jolene entered. Madam Charbonneau stood in front of her desk. She stared at Jolene for a moment, and then walking toward her, she gave Jolene the back of her hand. It was a hard blow, as powerful as any man. Jolene fell to the floor, blood trickling from the side of her mouth.

"Do you know how much money you cost me?" the woman shouted down at Jolene. "It's expensive to keep and teach a girl for as long as necessary. As well, I had to reimburse Mr. Runt for his losses. Now, I'm going to make my investment back with a profit. Knowing you, I imagine you're still a virgin. Gentlemen of quality and wealth will pay highly for a virgin. There are tricks I've learned over the years. I could sell you as a virgin five, six, maybe as many as ten times."

"I'll have nothing to do with it," Jolene said, looking up at her in defiance. "I will not give in to these men. I will be contrary in every way. I will fight them tooth and nail. I will bite, kick, and claw every moment till they realized the error of their ways."

With that, Madam Charbonneau burst into a fit of laugher. "You foolish girl, do you know how many men pay far more highly for a woman to fight their advances? It inflames their desire to a feverish pitch. They gladly pay double for a Fancy who will deceivingly act out the part of a contraire. For a Fancy such as you who are sincere in their rebellion, they will pay triple. I will make my money back in no time."

Jolene got to her knees to beg, "Madam, please, have pity on me. I have been through so much, have pity. I will work for you till the payment is made. I will work each day till my hands bleed."

Madam Charbonneau smiled. "I think I understand why they pay so much for such a Fancy as you. Your tearful pleading only makes it sweeter. You will do as I say, or die."

"Then, madam, let me die."

"Oh, you will do as I say, but first you will know what it is to die. And when I bring you back from the dead, you will obey me without question. You will beg for the privilege."

Madam Charbonneau opened the door. There were two guards waiting in the hallway.

"These gentlemen are here to bring you to your room. I hope you find it to your liking?" Looking at the guards, pointing to Jolene, she gave the order, "Take her away."

****

It was a small dark room under the house with walls and floors of gray stone, what most folks would use as a root cellar. In this case, it was used as a wine cellar. The walls were lined with dusty wine bottles. In the center of the room, resting atop two wooden sawhorses was a black oblong box – a coffin.

Try as she might, Jolene was no match for the two strong guards. They lifted her up, placed her in the coffin, slamming the lid down. To make matters worse, they nailed it shut.

"Sirs, have mercy," Jolene cried.

They ignored her. She heard them leave. She was alone.

At first, she struggled, punching, pushing, and kicking the lid, to no avail. In time, she tired, resting motionless. There was no difference between having her eyes closed or open, there was nothing except pitch-black darkness. The air was thick and hard to breathe. After only a few hours, she feared for her sanity. Her only hope was prayer.

Eventually, she lost all sense of time with no idea how much elapsed, if it were day or night. Try as she may, she couldn't hold it any longer, she soiled herself. This caused her skin irritation that worsened with each passing hour till it was like a burning fire.

Without food or drink, she became weak. This caused her to sleep for hours, which in its way was a blessing. Still, it brought her closer to death. She feared she might not wake up again.

After when she was sure days had passed, she no longer prayed silently in her mind. She cried aloud for heaven to intervene.

"Oh, Lord, look down with mercy on your miserable sinner. I know I am not worthy, but you are the only well I know where I can drink the waters that will take away my thirst, forever. I bear no malice to all those who have put me here. I pray for their souls. As you freed Paul from prison, set me free!"

"You are more like Lazarus," a soft voice seeped through the lid of the coffin

Jolene recognized who it was, immediately. It was Madam Charbonneau.

"Not like Paul who was in prison," Madam Charbonneau continued. "You are like Lazarus, dead in his grave, for three days in the land of the dead, rotting away. I can smell you through this cedar lid. You smell like decaying flesh.

"Lazarus waited on the Lord, only you wait on me. Only I can free you from your tomb. I will not do so till you agree to obey me."

Jolene began to recite aloud the twenty-third psalm, "The Lord is my Shepherd. I shall not want…"

"That's right," Madam Charbonneau laughed. "Cling till the very end. The harder you cling to your belief, the sweeter it will be when you let go."

"…and I will dwell in the house of the Lord, forever."

"Not forever, Jolene, just a few more days."

****

Jolene no longer slept, yet she remained unconscious. If not for the sweet cool air entering her lungs, she would not have known the lid of the coffin was removed. Strong arms carried her. She was placed in a tub, washed, dried, and dressed. When they laid her down on a bed, she fell into a deep sleep.

Over the next few days, with food and water, she became stronger. However, not strong enough to act or speak against Madam Charbonneau. All the fight was drained from her. She moved in whatever direction she was pointed, sat when made to sit, ate and drank when it was put before her, and slept when put to bed. Her will was no longer her own.

When she was able to sit up straight on her own, she began to have supper with Madam Charbonneau in her private dining room. However, they were never alone. Each night they dined with a different gentleman. It was clear, these men were very wealthy by the way they dressed and carried themselves. They were of different ages, though mostly they were older.

They ate very little, drinking heavily. The conversation, which was only between Madam and them was brief, always questions about Jolene.

"You guarantee she's a virgin?"

"You have my word, sir."

"Does she talk?"

"Why, is that necessary?"

They would laugh.

Jolene sat motionless, as if in a dream. Now and then she'd try to put food in her mouth, often it would fall from her fork to the floor.

On the third successive night of dinner in Madam's private dining room with an unknown gentleman, Jolene, in her daze, realized what was taking place. It was a drawn out auction for her.

Madam Charbonneau was putting her on the auction block. One by one, these men would get to inspect her. After a dozen or so of them had the chance to inspect the merchandise, each would send their bid to Madam Charbonneau, with Jolene going to the highest bidder.

"I'm not a virgin," Jolene murmured one night across the table to an elderly gentleman. "I was raped," she concluded.

Hearing this information, did not sway him. If anything, it fanned the flame of lust within him till it was a roaring inferno.

"I'll give you three thousand for her," the man implored Madam.

"Sir, please…"

"Leave the room this instant and I'll give you five thousand. I'll take her right here on this table."

"Sir, please, that wouldn't be fair to the other bidders. I'm afraid you will have to submit your bid and wait, like the others."

Madam Charbonneau couldn't expect things to go better if she'd written it all out as a play. Now, she had leverage to enhance the bidding. She wrote letters to each of the bidders.

Dear Mister X, Mister Y has already bid five thousand. Dear mister Y, Mister X has upped his bid over yours. Dear Mister Z, Misters X and Y have bid over seven thousand.

On and on it went, till the final bid was ten thousand. Mind you, this was only for one night. Madam Charbonneau planned to auction Jolene off at least four more times, in other cities, of course, least the clientele find out.

Twenty-Four

The Eyes of Casmir De La Fontaine

Casmir De La Fontaine was unanimously elected Commissioner General of Police for the city of New Orleans by the mayor and the city counsel ten years prior. He did not receive his position for any merit or experience on his part. Casmir knew nothing of police work or the law. They needed someone who would see things their way, take orders, keep his mouth shut, and not make waves. In short, they needed someone who was as corrupt as they. Still, why Casmir? Crooked politicians were under every rock. Casmir came from a wealthy family, and was willing to pay for the post.

Why would anyone pay such a high price for a position that paid a yearly allowance only one-tenth of what they paid for it? Because of the amount of money flowing under the table was an unstoppable tide. There were bribes, shady deals, and kickbacks, not to mention the laws you could break without worry of conviction.

The populous of the city knew of the corruption within city government and law enforcement. However, what could they do? As they say, *you can't fight city hall*. What good would it do to complain to a thief about how much he steals?

After ten years as Commissioner, Casmir De La Fontaine multiplied his wealth twentyfold. Now middle-aged, handsome by most standards, he remained unmarried, living in a magnificent two-story brownstone in town. He kept six house-staff living on the premises.

To say he lived alone would be a misinterpretation of the term *remained unmarried*. Seldom was there a night he did not have a bed companion. Usually, these were Fancy Girls, beautiful young black women. They were supplied to him at a discount for favors and to look the other way when necessary. Any friend of Casmir De La Fontaine could expect special treatment. The price of friendship was high; still it was well worth it.

For this reason, it was out of character for Casmir to bid so high for a Fancy Girl, as in the case of Jolene.

Excepting a dinner invitation from Madam Charbonneau, he sat across the table, his eyes fixed on Jolene, as if nothing else mattered in the world. That night he swore to have her.

As for the biding war that Madam Charbonneau caused with her letters in the post, Casmir ignored them. He submitted what he felt was a high enough bid to topple all the others. He was right.

The fuss that was made the day Jolene was to go to Casmir De La Fontaine's home was similar to a wedding night. They treated her like a bride, bathing her, perfuming her, and dressing her.

"You are his for the next twenty-four hours," Madam Charbonneau told Jolene as they stood out front of the gate. "He's paying a large sum for you. I do not want to lose any money. If you do not do as he instructs, if he is not satisfied, I will return you to your coffin, and this time there will be no resurrection."

Jolene was placed in the back of the carriage. "Make me proud," Madam warned as the carriage pulled away.

There was no response from Jolene. For the last few weeks, she remained in that dazed, dreamlike state. All sounds came from far away. Every vision was on a distant shore. She was inside herself, watching herself, watch herself.

The carriage barreled through the city till it came to a high hill overlooking the harbor. The drivers of the carriage were two guards from Madam Charbonneau. When they helped Jolene out of the cab, her first instinct was to bolt. Before she got three steps away, one of them grabbed her.

"Now, now, missy, we won't be havin' that," he said as the two guards took her by the arms, leading her to the front door.

"Ah, yes, we've been expecting ya," a little black man with gray hair, dressed in a black suit, said as he opened the front door.

"She'd like to run for it," said one of the guards. "I'd feel better if we delivered her ourselves."

"Very well, the master is in his study."

"Splendid...splendid..." Casmir proclaimed when they ushered Jolene into the study.

"We leave her in your good hands, sir," one of the guards stated. "We will be back in twenty-four hours to collect her."

"Yes…yes, very good. Now, please, leave," Casmir spurted, too busy eyeing Jolene to pay attention to anyone else.

When they left and the doors to the study closed, Casmir took Jolene in his arms, kissing her. She didn't fight back nor did she respond. She was like a wet rag in his arms. Sadly, it didn't seem to matter. It made no difference to him.

He poured them both a sherry, handing her the glass. "Drink, my dear, I have a most splendid evening planned for the both of us."

When she refused to drink, he held her mouth open, forcing it down her throat, causing her to choke. He poured her another. Realizing there was no escape, she drank it down.

In the dining room, they sat at a long table next to each other. The table was covered with exotic and costly dishes.

"Eat…eat!" he demanded.

She ate just enough to appease him, as gluttony opened its door to him. He ate frantically with his hands, chewing only once or twice before swallowing. All the while, he forced her to drink sherry and champagne till her head began swimming.

"Please, sir, let me go," Jolene said softly. "You are the Commissioner General of Police are you not? If you let me go, I will tell you of the many crimes I have witnessed."

"Such as," he asked, smiling, slurring his words.

"I know for a fact that Boniface Martin was not killed in a robbery. It was unadulterated murder."

Casmir laughed so hard he spilled his drink. "Oh, that," he bellowed. "You mean Dominique and Edmond, his son. I know all about that. I was paid well to look the other way on that one. Slandering my good friends will not gain your freedom."

Jolene sank even lower in herself. Were there any good men left? Had the entire world lost its soul?"

"Drink up," Casmir demanded, pouring her another glass.

When they were done, they were both drunk, he more than she. He took her by the arm, pulling her upstairs. The main bedroom was large and well decorated. To one wall was an overly-huge canopy bed. He sat down on the edge of the bed, smiling at her. There was a tray on the nightstand. On the tray was another bottle of sherry. He poured them both a glass.

"Please, I can't drink anymore," Jolene beseeched.

"Nonsense…the night is young. We haven't even begun," he said, spilling most of his drink. "Now, drink," he ordered.

Jolene forced it down.

The smile left his face. "Now…strip!" he demanded.

"Sir, please."

"Take off your clothes. I want to see what I paid so dearly for."

Jolene fell to her knees at his feet. "I beg you! Please, don't ask this of me. It is wrong. It is a sin against God and man. We are not animals. We have a soul. It is our responsibility to stay clean and worthy of heaven. I beg you to give up these thoughts and repent."

He stared at her in amazement. "That is fantastic," he proclaimed. "Oh, how it excites me to hear you speak this way. Promise me you will continue with this rant. I promise to pay an additional thousand to Madam Charbonneau, if you do." He pushed his foot into her face, slamming her to the floor. "Now, take off your clothes!" he insisted.

Jolene stood, in tears, she slowly undressed. When she stood naked before him, he rushed to her, holding her in his arms, kissing her. His hands moved over her like snakes. Grabbing her, he tossed her onto the bed. He ripped one of the sheets into strips. Using them, he tied her to the bedpost, a strip at each corner, her wrists and ankles. She lay naked, spread-eagle.

The next moment, he was on top of her, kissing her, moving his body as if trying to burrow through her. Then without warning, to her surprise, he stopped. He got off her, off the bed, and then walked out of the room, slamming the door shut.

This baffled Jolene; she had no idea what he could be up to.

A minute later, she heard a sound coming from the opposite wall. She raised her head just in time to see a small square of the wall being removed. From this gap in the wall, two eyes peered at her from the next room. There was no mistaking it; they were the eyes of Casmir De La Fontaine. Except now, there was madness in them only seen in wild animals. What was he up to?

The bedroom door opened. A man entered. He was a black man dressed in work-clothes. He was young and tall, a head above most men. His muscular arms branched out from his massive chest, as wide as a church door. He stood before the bed, looking down at Jolene. There was no expression on his face, just a cold stare. He slowly began to undress.

Completely naked, he fell down upon Jolene. His great weight made it impossible for her to move, and difficult to breathe.

"Please, in the name of God, have mercy on me. Don't do this," she cried into his neck.

He whispered in her ear, "He's watchin'. I'd like to help ya, but he's watchin.'"

Jolene cried all the more, burying her face in his neck.

He whispered, again, "Listen, if I free ya, ya gotta grab ya clothes. Don't waste time gettin' dressed. Just run for it."

This little light of hope stopped her from crying.

"Ya ready."

The next instant, he took hold of the strips holding her hands in place. He tore her free. Reaching down, he did the same, freeing her legs.

"Stop that…stop that…!" Casmir shouted through the small gap in the wall.

Jolene got out from under him, jumping off the bed.

"Stop her…stop her…!" Casmir hollered.

Jolene picked up her clothing from the floor, heading for the door. Just as she left the room, a gunshot exploded. She looks back to see the muzzle of a smoking gun sticking out of the gap in the wall. Another shot rang out, hitting the young man, again. He rolled off the bed, onto the floor. His back was bloody from the two gunshots. She stared down at him, not knowing what to do. Their eyes meet, sadness passed between them.

"Go…!" he cried as he collapsed face down on the floor.

Fear got the better of her. She ran down the stairs to the front door. Outside, she looked up and down the street. Thankfully, it was late and there wasn't anyone around. She ran down the street till she got to a wall. There, she hid within the shadows. First, she untied the strips from her hands and feet, and then she dressed, quickly. She had not been able to get her shoes. She ran barefoot.

She needed to hurry, they would be after her. At the top of a hill, she could see the harbor; she ran toward it.

Twenty-Five

The Next Morning

"Madam, the Commissioner General is here to see ya," one of the guards announced, standing in the doorway of Madam Charbonneau's office.

"Send him in."

A moment later, Casmir came bursting into the room.

"Ah, Casmir, bringing her back so soon?" Madam asked, smiling up at him.

"What…bring her back? She ran away, last night. I have no idea where she is."

"Do you have any of your men out looking for her?"

"Of course, as many as I could spare."

"I'll help you anyway that I can, Casmir."

"Well, you can start by giving me my money back."

Madam smiled, tilting her head. "Why do you say that?"

"I paid for twenty-four hours. She was barely at my home three hours."

"It's not my fault you let her go. Imagine, the Commissioner General of the Police, and you can't even hold onto a little girl. But I'll tell you what I'll do. I'd refund your money, only, you lost her, so you must pay for her. I could have easily sold her out for thousands of dollars many nights over. As I see it, you owe me a considerable amount of money."

"That's preposterous…!"

"Listen, Casmir, there's no reason for us to quarrel. We need to pool our resources, and find this girl."

Casmir thought for a moment. "You're right. Do you know how dangerous the girl is? She opened her mouth last night, admitting to knowing about certain crimes in the area. What I want to know is how she was able to live, if you knew about this?"

"I don't know what you're talking about," Madam said coldly.

"There are others who have a stake in this. I'm going to see them. We can use all the allies we can find."

With that, Casmir stormed out of Madam's office.

"Casmir, what are you doing here?" Edmond Martin asked.

"We need to talk, Edmond," Casmir replied.

"Go ahead, whatever you have to tell me; you can say in front of Dominique, you know that."

"It's about a girl I got from Madam Charbonneau. She said some things that were quite disturbing. She knew all about you and Dominique and your father."

"Where's the girl, now?"

"I have no idea. She ran off, last night."

"That is a problem," Edmond shook his head.

"What I don't understand is if the girl knew so much, why did you let her slip through your fingers?"

"You'd have to ask Dominique about that," Edmond responded, looking to Dominique.

"I don't see what the problem is. She's just another Fancy Girl. No one will ever listen to her or believe what she says, if she did speak."

Edmond smiled, seeing Dominique in a new light. "Now, I understand, you have a thing for this girl." He turned to Casmir. "You need to understand, my dearest here, has many tastes. She doesn't always know if she's coming or going, if she's a man or a woman," he laughed.

"This is no laughing matter," Casmir insisted. "This girl knows too much."

"Don't be silly," Dominique said, pouring them all a sherry. "All we need do is find this girl and…"

"And kill her," Casmir added.

"No, no, not at all," Dominique continued. "Don't you see how this furthers our purpose? We capture her, and bring her to trial. There are so many swords hanging over this girl's head, theft, murder. She will be found guilty with little effort. All we do is add the killing of Boniface to the list. She will hang for it, and we can rest easy."

"But she's innocent," Casmir argued.

"No one is going to believe a colored girl, especially a Fancy Girl. She won't be the first innocent soul to die for another's crime."

Twenty-Six

That Night

Even at such a late hour, the taverns along the waterfront were open and filled to capacity. Music bellowed out of each, fading as she strode on. The streets were busy, as well. As in the taverns, the streets were occupied mostly by sailors who set sail on the ships in the harbor. They were loud and drunk. A sailor needs only two reasons to drink. He just shipped in or he's just shipping out, which is the constant state sailors are in.

Wherever you find large groups of drunken sailors, you find ladies of the night, white and black. They lined the streets like the trees in the wealthy parts of town. The taverns were wall-to-wall with them. A few times, Jolene was approached. She kept her head down, continuing to walk on.

Perhaps, it was a mistake to come to the harbor. However, it was more likely they were hunting her on streets and roads leading out of the city. It didn't matter, now. She was alone on the harbor, desperately needing a place to hide.

As she walked on, she saw a woman walking down the street in the opposite direction, coming toward her. She was a tall, lanky black woman, clearly drunk and staggering. Without warning, the woman stepped into a cove in one of the buildings. As Jolene came closer she heard the woman heaving. Coming on her, she found the woman holding onto the wall, keeping her balance. Her back was to Jolene. The woman stiffened for a second and then fell to the ground in a faint, onto her own vomit.

"Are you all right?" Jolene asked, rushing to the woman.

"Just get me to my room, I'll be fine," she murmured.

"Where do you live?"

It took all her strength to answer. "626 Frenchman Street, just up the street, above the Black Swan Tavern, get me there and I'll be all right."

It was a struggle getting her up and walking, the woman was so weak and limp.

"I live here," she mumbled, pointing to stairs on the side of the building.

Jolene helped her up slowly, step by step. At the top, the door was open. It was a small, dark, shabby room with a bed in front of the only window, overlooking the street, beyond that was the harbor. The music, laughter, and chatter from the Black Swan Tavern below seeped through the floor, almost as loud as being in the tavern.

Jolene dropped the woman on the bed, flat on her back.

"Quick, get me something to be sick in," the woman said.

Jolene looked around the room; all she could find was a chamber pot. Putting it under the woman's chin, Jolene lifted her head. What little light penetrated the filthy window illuminated the woman's face. Jolene immediately recognized her.

"Rosiline...! Is it really you?" Jolene exclaimed.

Once she finished, Rosiline looked up from the chamber pot. "Jolene...how strange it is to see you."

"Rosiline, what happened to you?"

"The night Graham was shot, like you, the girls and I knew we had to get out of there before the police arrived. I packed as much as I could in a small bag and left." She went thoughtful for a moment. "I loved him. I loved Graham, despite whom and what he was."

"I understand," Jolene said, not wanting to speak of her own feelings for Graham.

"When I left the building, I had to walk around the body. Did you see him lying in the street?"

"Yes, I did," Jolene admitted sadly. "Rosiline, how sick are you?"

"I just need a few days rest; I'll be fine. If you have nowhere to go, you can stay here. I could use the company."

Jolene helped Rosiline undress and get under the covers.

"You just rest. We'll talk in the morning," Jolene said, wiping the sweat from Rosiline's forehead.

"Jolene...thank you," Rosiline whispered, closing her eyes.

Jolene took up the chamber pot to place it away in a corner. Walking past the window, a stream of light shown on the contents. Inside was a film of phlegm mixed with a large quantity of blood.

****

Days later, Rosiline was not any better, in fact, she was worse. With a wet rag, Jolene washed her a few times each day, trying to keep the fever down. Searching the room, she found a few coins to buy food. Rosiline ate very little.

"You need a doctor," Jolene finally admitted.

"No…no doctors," Rosiline insisted.

One night, Jolene heard the sound of heavy feet coming up the stairs. Jolene rushed to lock the door. The doorknob turned. When they couldn't open the door, they pounded on it.

"Why is this door locked," a man's voice roared. "Rosiline, it's me, open the door before I break it down."

Fearing the worst, Jolene unlocked the door. A large white man with dark curly hair, an unkempt beard, dressed in a torn black suit, entered.

"Who are you?" he asked Jolene, staring her down, then looking over to Rosiline lying on the bed. "What's wrong with her?"

"She hasn't been well," Jolene said, trying to stand between the man and the bed. "I'm an old friend of Rosiline. My name is Jolene. And you are…?"

"Never mind who I am. She knows who I am," he said, pushing Jolene out of the way. Standing over Rosiline, he shook her awake. "Rosiline, it's me. Where's my money?"

"I told you she hasn't been well," Jolene maintained firmly.

"I don't care if she's got one foot in the grave. She works for me, and she needs to be out on the streets."

"I'll be fine, tomorrow," Rosiline struggled to speak.

"What about the money you owe me, now!" he growled.

"I'll have it tomorrow and more."

The man looked at Jolene. She wore a thin golden necklace on which dangled a single pearl. He reached out, ripping it from her throat. He held it up to the light to inspect it.

"What's this? It ain't real, but it'll buy you another day. I'll be back tomorrow for the rest."

He headed for the door, turning back to give the two women one last look in anger. "Tomorrow," was his last warning.

Jolene held her breath, as she listened to him tramping down the stairs. She stood motionless until she was sure he was gone.

"What are we going to do?" Jolene asked.

"Help me up," Rosiline answered. With all her strength, she tried to rise off the bed, only to fall back down in tears.

****

That night, while Rosiline slept, Jolene took to the streets, begging. It was slow going, a penny here, a penny there. Many a sailor made propositions, all were indecent proposals. The thought of straying from what she knew to be morally right did cross her mind. After all, she believed it was a matter of life and death, Rosiline's life, and hopefully not her death. Still, she couldn't bring herself to cross that bridge.

She entered the Black Swan Tavern, moving about begging for whatever coin they could spare.

"Get her out of here," one of the men working behind the bar shouted over the dim.

"Why?" said one of the older men, putting his arms around her waist. "I must admit at times in my life I've been not liking colored folks. Only that's what goes on in my mind. There are parts of my body that couldn't tell black from white and when I'm drunk I can't tell front from back," he announced loudly, as he pulled her up against his body. The crowd of men laughed. Jolene tried to break free, only it was useless.

"Is it true what they say about ya people?" the man said, the laughter of the others prodding him on. "Ya know what I mean. They say ya people got that hot rhythm flowin' in ya veins. Prove me right or prove me wrong. Let's see ya dance."

He let go of her, pushing her to the center of the room. He tossed a gold coin to the musicians. "Blow the man down," he demanded.

The band went into full sway, all the sailors in the room sang along.

Come all ye young fellow that follow the sea
To my way hay, blow the man down
And pray pay attention and listen to me
Give me some time to blow the man down.

I'm a deepwater sailor just in from Hong Kong
To my way hay, blow the man down
If ya give me some grog, I'll sing ya a song
Give me sometime to blow the man down

"Lay aft" is the cry, to the break of the Poop
To my way hay, blow the man down
Or I'll help ya along with the toe of my boot
Give me some time to blow the man down.

Pay attention to order, now you one and all
To my way hay, blow the man down
For right there above you fly the Black Ball
Give me some time to blow the man down

Jolene did her best to keep up with the music, dancing as fast as she could, through her embarrassment. The crowd laughed, throwing pennies at her. When the music stopped, she gathered the coins from the floor. She kept her head down in shame as she walked out of the tavern.

Her pockets were bulging with coins, except it was only pennies. She knew she needed more. As the night waned, begging for spare coin became near unlikely. The drunks on the streets had nothing to offer except rude remarks.

There was a slight gold-blue tint on the edge of the sky. It would soon be morning. Jolene was just about to call it a night when she came upon a young sailor curled up in a ball in the same cove she found Rosiline in.

"Are you all right?" she asked him.

He grumbled in his drunkenness, barely able to make his words understood, his eyes heavy and closed.

A storm brewed inside Jolene's mind. She knew what was right and what was wrong. Still, she understood it might be a question of life or death if Rosiline had no money for the strange man, by the morning.

She reached out, slipping her hand into his jacket, finding his billfold. He was completely unaware. She quickly pulled away, pressing the billfold to her breast.

She rushed back to the apartment, she first checked on Rosiline. She was sleeping soundly. Jolene opened the billfold, counting it; she had doubled her money for the night. She held the bills in her hand, she began to cry.

"Is this the price of my soul? Oh, Lord, have mercy on me, a miserable sinner."

****

Almost to the minute, the burley man returned to the apartment. He held no sympathy for Rosiline, shouting at her.

"So, where's my money?"

She didn't even blink.

"Is she dead?" he asked Jolene.

"No, but she needs a doctor."

He ignored the comment, continuing to shout, "Where's my money?"

"Here it is," Jolene said, holding both hands full of coins and bills to him.

He took it from her. "I'm not a child!" he said angrily, placing the bills in his pocket and tossing the coins across the room. "Maybe you should work for me," he said, smiling at Jolene. He patted the pocket holding the bills. "This is enough to buy you another day," he said. "I'll be back tomorrow, I'll expect the same."

"That's impossible," Jolene cried. "Do you have any idea how difficult it was to get that much?"

"I don't really care; I only expect." Balling his fist, he punched Rosiline in the face, a blow for each word. "And...you...get...back...to...work!"

Jolene couldn't stop him. When he'd finished, Rosiline's face was battered and bruised, her lips and nose bled.

His last word as he left was the same as the day before, "Tomorrow!" which was a warning as well as a demand.

After he left, Jolene sat on the edge of the bed, cleaning Rosiline's wounds. The room darkened as the sun set. The carnival sounds of music and laughter from the Black Swan Tavern below began to grow louder. It was then Rosiline opened her eyes.

"You need a doctor," Jolene warned.

"It's too late for that," Rosiline whispered. "I'm sorry I've taken so long to die. You have been a kind friend. Stay awhile I will not be long. Tonight, I die."

"Don't say that," Jolene insisted. "There is always hope."

"Don't you understand? Jolene, listen to me. I want this. The road has been a long and tiring one. I've had my share of heartbreak. I look forward to dying, to leave this stinking world."

"You're wrong, Rosiline. It's a good world. God is good."

"Is he? If he does exist, which I doubt, he's either powerless or he doesn't care. Whatever the case may be, in the end it all works down to the same thing. It's an evil, merciless world, and I want out."

"That's blasphemy!" Jolene wept.

"How can you blaspheme what you don't believe exists. Jolene, you're a good person. The only good person I've ever known. One good person does not make a good world."

Jolene held Rosiline's hand.

"Push your hand under the mattress," she told Jolene. "Go ahead."

Jolene slipped her hand under the mattress. She removed her hand. It held a wad of bills.

"The night Graham died, everyone ran away before the authorities arrived. In the confusion, I scooped up all the money that was on the gambling table. No one seemed to miss it. They were too worried about their own skins. I've kept it all this time for a rainy day. Only now, there will be no more days, rainy or sunny. I want you to have it. Use it to get to a better place, wherever that may be, if it exists at all. Now, sit here with me, I don't want to die alone."

Rosiline closed her eyes. Jolene sat quietly on the edge of the bed holding her hand.

The room was pitch-black, now. The music and revelry coming from the tavern below was at full peak. Jolene could barely see the features of Rosiline's face, only the outline.

Jolene let go of Rosiline's hand. She fell to her knees at the side of the bed, bowed her head, praying softly, "Oh, Lord, look down upon your unworthy servant. I ask that you send down your grace on her soul. May she repent and except your grace. Have mercy on her soul."

With one last effort, Rosiline slowly sat up in bed. Jolene could only hope this was a sign from heaven – a miracle.

Rosiline sighed, and with her last breath she said, "Don't you dare ask God to help me!" She fell back onto the bed, and then she died.

Jolene fell to the floor in tears. The sound of singing blasted through the floor, filling her ears.

Pay attention to order, now you one and all
To my way hay, blow the man down
For right there above you fly the Black Ball
Give me some time to blow the man down

Twenty-Seven

Two Birds with One Stone

Not wanting to confront the authorities about poor Rosiline, she wrote a note about her passing, handing it to the barkeep at the Black Swan Tavern. Surely, the message would be passed on, and the body would be taken.

Jolene wandered alone along the harbor, the wad of money in her pocket, and a pair of Rosiline's shoes on her feet.

She thought about working her way through the city, to the outskirts, and finally back to the open road. Then it dawned on her there was more than one way to leave New Orleans behind. Ships were constantly coming and going. Passage on one of these ships would be swift and she would leave unseen.

It was the same with every ship she approached. Some would not allow her to board, having nothing to do with her. Others would not allow her to speak to anyone of authority, and would escort her away from the ship. In the few cases where she did get onboard and speak to someone who made such decisions, she was asked to leave or literally thrown off the ship.

Most assumed she was a runaway slave who'd robbed money from her master before escaping. They wanted nothing to do with her. Not that they were law-abiding, the money simple wasn't enough to take the chance.

When night came, she was tired and hungry. At the far end of the harbor was one last ship she hadn't tried, the *Sea Wolf*.

Stepping onboard, Jolene was confused. She understood the late hour; however this did not explain why no one was on deck. It seemed deserted.

"Hello," Jolene called out.

Except for the breeze moving and the water splashing against the side of the ship, all was silent.

"What ye be doin' here?" a voice called from behind her.

She spun around, fearfully, to be confronted with a pale, white-haired old man. His white beard was close-cropped, what could be described as just being unshaven. His dress was typical sailor attire, the flared pants and tight-knit stripped shirt. There was a half-full bottle of whiskey in his hand. His eyes were red from drink; still he swayed with the rocking of the ship as naturally as breathing.

"Where is everyone?" Jolene asked.

"Hold on there, missy," he slurred his words. "Ye come onboard, unannounced, and start askin' questions, it is I who gets to ask the questions. Who ye be, and state your business."

"My name is Jolene. I need to speak with the captain. I seek passage."

"Runaway, is ye?"

Jolene didn't answer; he assumed her silence to be a yes.

He took a long swig from his bottle. "Ye be one stupid girl," he laughed. "Can't ye see our flag? We be just come to port this day, not shippin' out. We made a long time of it around the Cape of Good Hope to India for tea, and all the way back round the Cape, and back, again. The captain ain't here. None of 'em is. They're all out stretchin' their legs. Not me, I ain't much for dry land."

"What is your name, sir?" Jolene asked.

"The name's William Crisp. Folks calls me Crispy. I don't mind." He took another swig. "This here's the Sea Wolf ye be on. And we ain't taken on no runaways at any price." Then he thought for a moment. "How much does ye have?"

Jolene held up the wad of bills. He reached out for it. Jolene pulled away, only she was too slow. He took hold of the money.

"Don't look like much," he said. "Not enough for a captain to put his hide on the line for. Don't forget he'd have to share with others. That makes the takes all the less."

"Well, then I'm sorry to bother you, sir," Jolene said, reaching for her money.

"Now hold on," he called out to her. "It not be enough for a captain. It is enough for an old salt like me-self, though."

He took the last sip from his bottle. Seeing it was empty, he tossed it overboard. It splashed in the water.

"I got me an idea. Follow me," he said, staggering off.

She followed him down a flight of stairs leading to the lower level. She knew she needed to be cautious, nevertheless she was desperate. Besides, he was far too drunk and old to put up much of a fight.

"This is where's we sleep," he said, pointing all around, and then leading down another flight to what could only be described as storage. There were large sacks of tea and large long crates. The aroma of tea leaves permeated the air.

"This be all of it. It all gets unloaded in the morning and taken to warehouses around town and a few places outside the city. It be the responsibility of yours truly to see that it gets to the correct destinations. Now, for the price of the handful ye got, I'll see to it ye get sent to the farthest delivery."

"How…?" Jolene asked.

Crispy took up a crowbar, using it to pry open one of the crates. It contained four large sacks of tea.

"We just takes out the sacks and put ye in. Ye look about the same weight. Nobody would know the wiser."

It sounded impossible, foolish, and even comical. Still, Jolene couldn't think of any alternative. If all went well, she'd be miles from the city.

"Well, what ye say?"

"Very well," Jolene said reluctantly.

He pocketed the money, and then took the sacks out of the crate, tossing them aside.

"All right, then, get on in."

Jolene stepped into the crate, and then lay flat.

"Whatever ye do, don't move or make a sound," he warned, placing the lid back on. Using the crowbar, he hammered the nail back into place. "Don't worry. By tomorrow afternoon, you'll be miles away," he whispered through the lid. Then there was a thud. He'd fallen asleep on top of the crate. Jolene heard him snoring. She wondered if she were doing the right thing. Was he so drunk he wouldn't remember what he did the night before?

Lying in the dark reminded her of being nailed into the coffin, so long ago, again waiting for resurrection.

****

Jolene woke to the sound of men shouting. It was the morning; they were unloading the crates off the ship. She heard them all around, huffing and puffing, moving the loads. When they took hold of the crate she was in, she tried her best not to move or make a sound. When they lifted the crate up by ropes and pulleys, it felt like she was floating weightlessly. They lowered the crate onto the pier with a thud.

She heard the voice of Crispy giving orders. The crates were lifted onto wagons. Jolene heard the sound of horse's hooves against the cobblestones as they moved through the city.

Every so often, the wagon would stop. The sound of men unloading some of the crates could be heard. When they finished, the wagon continued.

Eventually, the clomping of hooves on cobblestones stopped. There was the sound of wagon wheels rolling over dirt roads. They were out of the city.

During one of the stops, Crispy whispered through the lid to her. "Just two more deliveries and I can set ye free."

This gave Jolene new hope. Perhaps this wild plan was going to work?

There were two more stops. Jolene remained quiet and hopeful.

"Just another hour," she heard Crispy whisper.

Indeed, approximately an hour later the wagon came to a halt. She felt the crate being taken off the wagon and taken inside. From the sounds around her, she could tell it was inside a building.

"Wait for me outside," she heard Crispy order, after which she heard the tramp of two men leaving. All became silent.

The next moment, the squeal of nails against wood resonated, as Crispy pried off the lid.

It felt good to fell the cool air once again fill her lungs. She had been in darkness for so many hours; the light blinded her for a moment. When her sight cleared, she looked up to see the smiling face of Crispy. She smiled back up at him.

Trying to stand was difficult. Lying motionless for so long drained much of the blood and feeling out of her legs. Once on her feet, she looked around. She was in a room, a familiar looking room. Crispy stood before her, standing behind him, smiling as well, were the last four people Jolene expected to see.

Standing next to Crispy was Dominique, Edmond Martin, Madam Charbonneau, and the Commissioner of Police, Casmir De La Fontaine.

"You've done well, Crisp. Here is the rest of your money," Casmir said, handing money to Crispy.

"Thanks, Captain," he said tipping his cap. "Sorry about this, missy," he said to Jolene before he left the room.

"Get out of that box," Casmir ordered Jolene.

She stood silent in front of her capturers.

"Jolene, you have been such a disappointment," Dominique said, shaking her head.

"A thorn in our side," Edmond added.

"Not to mention a costly one," Madam concluded.

"It would be better for all of us if you were dead," Casmir said. "We could easily kill you this instant. Only we have a better plan."

"Edmond Martin has purchased you from me," Madam said. "So, I loose no money. It matters not what happens to you, now."

"Being your new owner, I give you as a gift to De La Fontaine," Edmond continued the story.

Casmir took it from there. "You are under arrest for the atrocities you blame on all these good people, and others I'm sure you're aware of, and some I'm sure you're not. You will be tried, found guilty, and hanged. Two birds with one stone. All suspicions of crime committed by us will be proven false and forgotten. And best of all, you the disappointing, costly, thorn in our sides will be removed."

Twenty-Eight

False Witness

No chances were taken. Casmir had three men with him for assistance in Jolene's arrest and transport to New Orleans. Her hands were cuffed and her legs shackled. She was placed in a carriage that was completely enclosed, only a small barred window in the one door of the carriage. Two of the men rode in the back with her, while Casmir and the driver rode on top.

It was a long ride to the city. The temperature in the cab soared. All of them sweat in silence, never speaking to her, she to them, or to each other.

It started to rain, which cooled down the cab. Jolene heard the rain on the roof. From the tiny back window, she could see the downpour and the dark sky off in the distance.

From the sound of hooves on the cobblestones, she knew they were back in New Orleans, without even looking. The carriage halted. The rain came down so hard, by the time they'd taken her from the carriage into the jail, she was soaked.

They placed her in a small single cell with just enough room to stand next to a cot. There was a bucket for private use against the far wall. And so it started, the long wait for the long arm of justice to come down on her as promised.

The days were sweltering, the nights were chilled. Jolene walked the length of the cell for hours, to stay limber and for something to do. No one visited her, except the guards who brought her two meals a day, and to empty her bucket once a week. She was given a wet towel every few days to wash herself. Her clothing was never cleaned or changed.

Weeks passed. When Jolene started to believe she'd been forgotten, the cell door opened. Two guards cuffed and shackled her. They escorted her down the hall and up the stairs to the courthouse, which was in the same building.

There were few people in the courtroom. There would be no jury; such things were not for runaways. The outcome was in the hands of the judge.

The Presiding Judge was the Honorable Renault Lamar. An old man with long white hair, steel gray eyes, a stooped back, and a crimson, bulbous drinker's nose.

Jolene sat before the judge's bench. Nearby was the prosecutor. There was no one assigned for her defense. It became immediately evident no one, not even herself, was to speak on her behalf.

One by one, people Jolene never knew or recognized were brought up to the witness stand to bear witness against her. She watched in amazement as they were sworn in, their right hand upon the Bible. What kind of people would swear on a Bible not to lie and then lie about someone they never knew? Surely, they were paid for their services. Jolene was compelled to pray silently for them. Love thy enemies is the rule, Jolene was surrounded by enemies, without a friend in sight.

After each witness stepped down, Judge Lamar would duck down under the judicial bench. He was a sloppy drinker. Everyone heard him guzzling. As the morning wore on, Judge Lamar became drunker.

"Court will stop for lunch, we will resume in an hour," Judge Lamar announced at fifteen minutes to noon.

There were actually more witnesses to be heard. They were taking no chance. They wanted a death sentence.

Jolene was taken back to her cell. She remained cuffed and shackled, and was given no food. She spent the hour on her knees, praying.

That afternoon was more of the same. Unknown witnesses were sworn in to give their testimony. Their stories sounded similar in many ways. Sometimes the same words and phrases were used. They were given a script to memorize, keep to, and recite.

They spoke about crimes such as the theft of Madam and Monsieur La Pire, the murders of the Reverend Osborne, Mrs. Lange, Georgette La Tueur, and Graham Dorsey. All false accusations, compiled with other crimes that were impossible for Jolene to have committed.

By the end of the day, it was clear to all Jolene was a murderer and a thief to the extent she was a one-woman crime spree.

Jolene still waited to tell her story; it was not to be. There seemed to be no reason to go any further. She was sure to be convicted and sentenced to the full extent of the law.

Two guards took hold of Jolene, leading her to stand before the judicial bench. Judge Lamar disappeared under the bench for one last drink before sentencing.

Sitting up as straight as he could, Judge Lamar spoke loud and clear for all to hear, "Jolene Fairchild you have been…"

"Do I not get my say?" Jolene asked.

Judge Lamar continued as if nothing happened. "Jolene Fairchild you have been found by this court..."

"How can you judge from only one side of the story?" Jolene shouted.

Again, he ignored her. "Jolene Fairchild..."

Jolene turned facing her accusers, "Thou shall not bear false witness!"

They looked at her as a woman gone mad.

Judge Lamar had enough. He pointed to one of the guards who knew exactly what needed to be done. One of the guards held her still, while another placed a gag across her mouth.

"Jolene Fairchild you have been found by this court to be guilty of crimes against the laws of the state of Louisiana and society. You are a thief and a cold-hearted murderer. You are sentenced to be hanged till you are dead within the next twenty-four hours. May God have mercy on your soul."

****

Late that night, Jolene couldn't sleep. A face appeared in the window of the cell door. It was Dominique.

"You have no idea what you've thrown away," she whispered to Jolene in a sad and serious tone.

"I could say the same about you," Jolene replied.

"Ah, you're still on that. Will you ever learn? Look around you. Is this what your God wants for you? Does He want you to suffer and die needlessly?"

"He wants me to live righteously."

"It's too late, Jolene. We could have been happy together. Once we got rid of Edmond it would all have been ours."

Jolene looked up into Dominique's face. There were tears running down her cheeks.

"Dominique...I will pray for you."

"You foolish girl, if you must pray then pray for yourself."

Twenty-Nine

An Acceptable Minimum

Jolene found it impossible to sleep, her mind was racing. The night was long, slow, and cold.

In the morning, after her bread and water, she was visited by two men. They weren't guards and didn't look like police. They were dressed plainly in business suits. One was tall, an older gentlemen with pompous air about him. He was clearly the one in charge. The other man was young, shorter, carrying items under his arm.

"Stand up," the older man ordered Jolene as they entered the cell.

Jolene looked at them with no response.

"I said, 'stand up'," he insisted. "Make her stand up," he ordered the younger man.

"You need to stand up," the younger man said, taking hold of Jolene's arm, helping her to her feet. He placed the items that he held down on the bed.

"Check her height," the old man said.

The younger man took up a tape measure from off the bed. Letting it roll out, he held it against Jolene.

"Stand up straight," he said.

She complied.

"One-hundred, seventy-five, point, twenty-six," the young man announced.

The older man wrote down the measurement in a small notepad.

The young man took up a square item, placing on the floor.

"Stand on this," he told Jolene.

She looked at him, questioning.

"Don't worry; it's just a spring scale. We need to know your weight."

Jolene stepped forward, standing on the square.

The young man looked down at the dial. "Eight point forty-three stone..."

The older man wrote down the number.

"You can get off it, now," the young man told Jolene, bending down to pick up the square. He gathered all the other items off the bed, putting them once more under his arm.

The older gentleman spoke softly. "My name is Quentin Munson, and this is my young protégé, Oliver Rigby. I can only image what is going through that pretty little head of yours at this moment, you poor dear. But, I want you to know you're in good hands. In fact, you are in the hands of the best."

Jolene seemed confused.

"I am thorough. I will keep the unpleasantness down to an acceptable minimum."

All the while, the young Mr. Rigby stood behind his mentor smiling and bobbing his head up and down with pride in agreement.

Mr. Munson continued, "Hanging does not have to be a painful experience. If all goes well, at the end of a long drop your neck will snap. Your death will be instantaneous and painless."

"And if I'm not lucky?" Jolene asked.

This question seemed to annoy both men.

Still, Mr. Munson gave his answer, "I wouldn't worry about that, if I were you. Like I said, you are in the best of hands."

This made the smile return to Mr. Rigby's face.

"But if you must know. If your neck doesn't break on impact, the pressure around your neck from the rope will block all blood coming from and going to the brain. There will be no air in the lungs. When the blood backs up, causing pressure, your capillaries will burst. Your heart rate will plummet. You will be dead in ten minutes. In short, you will strangle to death."

He knocked on the door, a guard opened it.

As they walked out, Mr. Munson gave his exiting remark, "Have no fear. You are in the best of hands."

"All the best," Mr. Rigby said, smiling, as the door slammed shut.

****

The door of the cell slowly opened. A guard entered, one Jolene never saw before. He was young and handsome with sandy blonde hair and sky-blue eyes. He was tall and slender. His Adam's apple protruded nearly as far as his chin. He wore an awkward smile.

"How are you holdin' up?" he asked.

Jolene thought this an odd question to ask of someone scheduled to die in only a few hours. Still, his smile and the innocent look on his face made her feel comfortable.

"I'm just fine. Thank you for asking."

"I'd be scared senseless. You're not scared!"

Jolene looked at him strangely.

"Oh, I'm sorry," he said. "My name's Paul Turner, I'm one of the new guards, here. If you don't want to talk about it, I'll understand. I'm here to see what you'd like for your last meal. You can have anything you want, within reason, of course."

Jolene didn't have to think twice.

"When I was a little girl, my mother would serve us peaches and cream with a sprinkle of sugar on top."

"I don't know if we have any peaches, I know we got cream and sugar, but I don't know about the peaches."

"If you can't, that's all right. It was just a thought," Jolene said softly.

Paul smiled, turned and left, closing the cell door gently.

Hours passed, Jolene assumed her last meal was impossible to present or Paul forgot about her. At that moment, the cell door opened. Paul entered holding a bowl and a spoon; he handed them to Jolene. It was her peaches and cream with a sprinkle of sugar.

"Thank you, that's very kind of you," Jolene said.

"You're welcome," Paul said, turning for the door.

"No, I'm not," Jolene called to him. He turned to look at her. "No, I'm not scared. I know where I'm going. I have no fear."

"Gee," was all he could say. He thought for a minute. "You must be a real good person."

"I wish I was," Jolene answered.

"Well, I'll be back later for the bowl," he smiled and left.

An hour later, the cell door opened. In walked one of the guards, a grumpy old man who wore his uniform in a haphazardly manner. He needed a shave. His hair had not been combed. It was evident he'd eaten onions with his supper. He reached out, Jolene handed him the empty bowl and spoon.

"Where's Paul?" she asked.

"Paul...who?" he asked, looking at her confused.

"The young man who was here earlier, he brought me this bowl."

"Oh, him, we won't be seein' him around here anymore."

"Why not...?"

"They fired him, tonight. Stupid kid got caught stealin' peaches off a tree down the road. Nope, won't see him, again."

He left, slamming the cell door closed.

****

It was impossible for Jolene to get any sleep. Thoughts and prayers flooded her mind; still it did not seem to affect her. She'd never felt so awake in her life.

It was early morning just hours before her execution. The cell door slowly opened. In stepped a priest, clearly so by his brown cassock and knotted rope sash with a rosary at his side.

"I'm Father Salvador. I'm here to hear your confession."

He was a round little man, made to look more so by his garb, dark hair and eyes, a tight cropped beard that came to a point at his chin. He wore a solemn face expressing the seriousness of the moment. He moved in closer.

"Is there something you'd like to confess?"

"No, sir, there is nothing."

A worried look came upon him. "My child, you have little time on this earth. You will be meeting your maker within the hour."

"Thank you, sir, but there is nothing."

"Surely you must have sinned in your life, my child?"

"Yes, I have, many times and everyday. Only they are nothing the Lord doesn't already know about and has forgiven."

"How can sin be forgiven without penance?"

"Oh, there was penance, paid in full by the Lord himself. If I were to confess my sins and do penance, I would be throwing the gift of Grace back in his face. No, sir, I have nothing to confess."

"I will pray for your soul."

"Thank you, sir, and I will pray for you."

****

"Stand up," one of four guards ordered as they entered the cell.

They cuffed and shackled Jolene, and then guided her out of the cell. Walking down the hall, they passed the stairs leading up to the courthouse. They continued down the hall, turning left toward a closed metal door. On opening the door, Jolene was blinded by sunlight. They walked out to a courtyard. In the center of the clearing was a gallows.

Dozens of people were there, authorities, reporters, no one Jolene knew. They moved through the crowd to the scaffold. People whispered as they walked by. All eyes staring at her, following her every move.

The scaffold was tall with a staircase leading to the top. At the foot of the scaffold, they stopped for a moment. Jolene looked up to see Quentin Munson at the top, a secure comforting look on his face. His protégé Oliver Rigby stood behind him, looking down with sad doe eyes.

The stairs were not wide enough for any more than two to walk up at a time. Like a father walking his daughter down the aisle, one of the guards took her by the arm guiding her up the thirteen steps, followed by the other guards.

Munson greeted her at the top, moving her to the center of the landing, standing over a trapdoor. They took off the cuffs and shackles, replacing them with wide leather straps, one binding her hands behind her back, the other tightly around her ankles.

Munson placed the hangman's noose around her neck, pulling it tight to one side.

"Remember what I said," Monson whispered. "There's nothing to worry about. You're in the best of hands."

He backed away. Rigby stepped forward, holding a black sack to place over her head.

Before he could, Jolene moved her head, shouting, "Wait, don't I get to say any last words?"

Rigby looked around, helplessly, for someone to make the call.

"No one cares what you've got to say," one of the guards said. "Proceed with the hangin'," he ordered.

"Sorry," Rigby said softly. He gently placed the sack over her head. The world went black.

Thirty

Innocence

All Jolene could hear was the pounding of her heart throbbing in her ears, as she stared into the darkness all around.

"Stop...stop...don't do anything. No one move!" a voice was heard.

The mumbling of the crowd below rose to meet her, then the sound of someone running up the stairs of the gallows.

"Here, read this," someone said.

Jolene's hearing was so acute at that moment, she heard someone unfolding a sheet of paper.

"Undo her," one of the guards said.

First they moved her off the trapdoor, removed the sack from off her head. She breathed in sweet air. Munson removed the noose as Rigby undid the straps. The guards cuffed and shackled her. The crowd chattered as they took her down, into the building, and back to her cell. Jolene was too upset to speak.

Hours later, the cell door opened. This time they didn't bother to cuff and shackle her. The guard walked her down the hall, passed the stairs that led to the courthouse, passed the door leading to the gallows, taking a left, through a door opening to the street. There, the secure carriage that brought her to the jail was waiting for her. They gently placed her in the back. Jolene was confused and frightened. She didn't ask any questions, afraid it was all too good to be happening. Truly, the hand of the Lord was in on this.

They drove for an hour, far from the city, arriving at a large three-story mansion. They escorted Jolene to the front door, and knocked. A moment later, a butler in a fine dark suit answered.

"Ah, yes, we've been expecting you. I can take her from here."

The guards released Jolene. The butler gently guided her inside, closing the door behind them.

Immediately, Jolene was taken by the breathtaking beauty of her surroundings. The greeting hall was two-stories high. The floor was black marble with such a deep shine it was like walking on mirrors. The walls were covered with paintings from the renaissance. Before them was a winding staircase leading to the second and third floor.

"What is this all about?" Jolene finally had to ask.

"It's not for me to say. All will become clear in a moment. Please, follow me."

Jolene followed him into a room at the far right. With just one look around, she realized she was in a library. It was a large room with shelves of books all about. In front of a floor to ceiling window was a large desk. Before it a world globe on a pedestal. To the right was a fireplace. On the mantle were more books. In the center of the room were two sofas facing each other. Sitting alone on one of the sofas facing her was a well-dressed gentleman. He stood as she entered.

"Please, come in," he said, smiling. "That will be all for now," he told the servant who turned and left. "Please, sit down," he said, pointing to the sofa facing his.

Jolene cautiously walked to the center of the room, facing him.

"Please, sit down," he repeated.

He was the most elegant white man Jolene ever met. His grooming and chiseled good-looks were striking. His smile was welcoming and sincere. Still a young man, there was a small amount of salt and pepper in his hair.

He remained standing, only taking his seat once Jolene did.

"I'm sure you have a thousand questions," he laughed. "Let me start at the beginning. My name is Jonathan Gibbs. I am the City Judge. One of the duties of a City Judge is to oversee the rulings of the Municipal Court. You were tried in a Municipal Court. I have the jurisdiction to override any of their rulings, which I've down in your favor."

Jolene was baffled. "Why would you do that?"

"Because I believe you are innocent."

"Why would you think that?"

He laughed. "Actually, it wasn't me, it was my wife. She sat in on the trial the entire day. She listened to your accusers. She believes it was all false accusations. She believes you are not guilty. I must admit she has a way of seeing through such things. I trust her judgment. But first, tell me in your own words."

For the next hour, Jolene relayed every major moment in her life starting from when she was taken from her home up to the moment a noose was placed around her neck. She told him about her time spent at Madam Charbonneau's, and of her escape. She confessed to the accidental killing of Reverend Osborne, being falsely accused of theft by Madam and Monsieur La Pire. She told him how she fell in with a bad crowd, led by Dominique. As she spoke about her love for Graham Dorsey, she broke down in tears. On and on she conveyed the long list of misfortunes that plagued her life.

When she'd finished, they both sat silently.

"I am innocent of all wrongdoing, sir, I swear."

"No need to swear. I believe you. Now that I've heard it from your lips, it only confirms what my wife has told me all along." He stood up and pointed behind Jolene. "Ah, here is my wife, now."

Jolene turned to see a woman as elegant as her husband. Her dark hair was done up like a crown, every hair in place. She was dressed in a gown made for a princess. Her bare shoulders set off the diamond necklace around her neck. Diamonds sparkled from nearly every finger.

She stood next to her husband. "Did I not tell you, my darling, she was innocent," she said, leaning forward, kissing his cheek.

"Yes, you did, my dear," he confirmed.

They both sat down, facing Jolene. The woman's eyes looked into Jolene's. They began to well up with tears. She reached across, taking Jolene by the hand.

"Has it been that long? Do you not recognize your sister?"

Jolene leaned forward, searching the woman's face.

"Winnie!" she cried.

"Yes, but no longer Winnie. I'm now Mrs. Gibbs," she said, smiling at her husband. "I've worried about you everyday since the night I helped you over the wall of Madam Charbonneau's school. You were the sister I never had. I'm so sorry for all you've gone through. If only I'd been there. But all that will change from this day forward." She turned to Jonathon, "She can stay with us?"

"Of course, if that makes you happy," he replied with a smile.

"Yes, it would." She stood up, still holding Jolene's hand. "Oh, my dear sister…"

Jolene jumped to her feet. The two women hugged, holding each other in tears.

****

Some may call it coincidence, others a miracle. For Jolene, life finally became good. Her happiness knew no bounds. As for her joy, it was there from the beginning and would remain with her till the day she died. Nothing or no one could have ever taken it away from her. It is a joy only found in the heart.

THE END

Michael Edwin Q. is available for book interviews and personal appearances. For more information contact:

Michael Edwin Q.
C/O Advantage Books
P.O. Box 160847
Altamonte Springs, FL 32716
michaeledwinq.com

Other Titles in this series by Michael Edwin Q:

Born A Colored Girl: 978-1-59755-478-4
Pappy Moses' Peanut Plantation: 978-1-59755-482-8
But Have Not Love: 978-1-59755-494-7
Tame the Savage Heart: 978-1-59755-5098
A Slaves Song: 978-1-59755-527-5

To purchase additional copies of these book visit our bookstore website at:
www.advbookstore.com

Longwood, Florida, USA
"we bring dreams to life"™
www.advbookstore.com